The Secret
at
Haney Field

Twelve-year-old April O'Day's summer has gotten off to a flying start. As the new bat retriever for the Harpoons, her hometown's minor-league team, she's fetching bats and doling out great advice to players and coaches alike. In a word, she's becoming indispensable. But mysterious things are happening at Haney Field, which April and her best friend—and fellow baseball enthusiast—Darren Plummer are determined to uncover. As they quickly learn, this is no ordinary season. In fact, it's a whole new ballgame!

Praise for *The Secret at Haney Field*

". . . a well-written Disney-like story. . . . The characters are well-drawn and likable, and Clark obviously knows baseball . . . . A home run. . . ."   —*Kirkus Reviews*

"Told in first person by April, her experiences are an inviting read. The discoveries and the reflections of this feisty protagonist, who loves the sport and whose curiosity leads her to investigate the Negro leagues, baseball history, and even issues of discrimination, are what make this story so enjoyable. . . ."
—*Diane Donovan, Midwest Book Review*

"April is a likeable and engaging heroine and Darren is good comic relief. The writing is clear and fluid, the dialogue smooth and realistic, and the baseball know-how is very interesting!"   —*Julia Hopkinson for Readers' Favorite*

"As deeply moving as *Field of Dreams*. . . . Inspiring, intriguing, and insightful. . . ."   —*Bil Howard for Readers' Favorite*

"R. M. Clark's baseball mystery . . . will royally entertain baseball fans of all ages. . . . This book is great fun and highly recommended."   —*Jack Magnus for Readers' Favorite*

The *Secret*
at
Haney Field

A BASEBALL MYSTERY

R. M. Clark

MB PUBLISHING

ISBNs:
Softcover: 978-0-9913646-2-6
Epub: 978-0-9913646-3-3
Kindle: 978-0-9913646-4-0
Library of Congress Control Number: 2014902495

Photo & Illustration Credits
Cover image: Hu Jingran © 123RF.com
Title page and chapter opener image: © iStockphoto.com/AtomA

Page 15: "There's no crying in baseball": From *A League of Their Own*, the 1992
Penny Marshall film.

To Sandy,
my best friend

Glossary

Bullpen: A warm-up area for pitchers and catchers. It is typically located behind the left or right base line or an outfield fence.

Bunt: Purposely batting the ball weakly to a specific spot on the infield by holding the bat still and letting the ball hit it. When used to advance base runners, where the only play by an infielder is to throw the batter out at first base, the maneuver is called a **sacrifice bunt.** If, however, the infielders are playing back and the batter is a speedy runner, then a bunt can be used to get a base hit.

Clean-Up Hitter: As the fourth player in the **lineup** (i.e., the list of players in the order in which they will bat), this batter is usually the team's best power hitter. If any of the first three batters gets on base, the No. 4 hitter ideally "cleans up" the bases with a hit, potentially driving in a run (or runs).

Cut-Off: A defensive tactic, whereby an infielder (usually, the first baseman, the second baseman, or the shortstop) catches the ball that is thrown in by an outfielder and then, quickly, throws it to the third baseman or the catcher at home plate to keep a runner (or runners) from advancing or scoring.

Double: The batter arrives safely at second base.

Doubleheader: Two games played by the same two teams on the same day.

Fastball: The most common pitch, it is a straight pitch that is thrown at a pitcher's top speed. A fastball that breaks slightly downward over the plate is called a **two-seamer** or a **sinker.**

Compare to a **breaking ball:** A pitch that deviates from a straight path by changing direction as it approaches the plate—either diving sharply over the plate (i.e., a **curveball**) or dropping down and across the plate (i.e., a **slider**).

Glove/Mitt: A leather covering for the hand used to catch a baseball. It has individual thumb and finger sections. Catchers and first basemen wear gloves called mitts (designed in the style of a mitten).

Grand Slam: A home run that is hit with the bases loaded (i.e., there is a runner on each base—first, second, and third). In a grand slam, four runs are scored.

Infield: The positions played by four players: the first baseman, the second baseman, the third baseman, and the shortstop (the shortstop covers the area between second base and third base). It's also the area of the field that's within and around home plate, first base, second base, and third base.

Line Drive: A line drive is a batted ball that is hit low to the ground in a nearly straight line.

Major Leagues: This name refers to the organization that operates the two North American professional baseball leagues—the **American League** (Baltimore Orioles, Boston Red Sox, Chicago White Sox, Cleveland Indians, Detroit Tigers, Houston Astros, Kansas City Royals, Los Angeles Angels, Minnesota Twins, New York Yankees, Oakland Athletics, Seattle Mariners, Tampa Bay Rays, Texas Rangers, and Toronto Blue Jays) and the **National League** (Arizona Diamondbacks, Atlanta Braves, Chicago Cubs, Cincinnati Reds, Colorado Rockies, Los Angeles Dodgers, Miami Marlins, Milwaukee Brewers, New York Mets, Philadelphia Phillies, Pittsburgh Pirates, San Diego Padres, San Francisco Giants, St. Louis Cardinals, and Washington Nationals). Learn more at baseballhall.org (the National Baseball Hall of Fame and Museum).

Minor Leagues: Composed of 240 professional baseball teams in the Americas, the six leagues, from Rookie to Triple-A, compete below the level of Major League Baseball and provide opportunities for players to prepare themselves for the major leagues.

Missed Signs: Hand or body signals given by the coach or the key players that are not followed correctly by the player being signaled.

Negro Leagues: From 1920–1960, 73 teams operated within 8 U. S. professional baseball leagues (i.e., the Negro National League [1920–1931], the Southern Negro League [1920], the Eastern Colored League [1923–1928], the Negro Southern League [1926, 1932, 1945], the American Negro League [1929], the East-West League [1932], the Negro National League [1933–1948], and the Negro American League [1937–1960]) in Alabama, Arkansas, Delaware, District of Columbia, Florida, Georgia, Illinois, Indiana, Kentucky, Louisiana, Maryland, Michigan, Missouri, New Jersey, New York, Ohio, Pennsylvania, Tennessee, and Texas. Learn more about the Negro Leagues at nlbm.com (the Negro Leagues Baseball Museum).

On-Deck Circle: Five feet in diameter, this circular area on the field (in foul territory, about halfway between the team's dugout and home plate) is where the next batter in the lineup takes warm-up swings before going to the batter's box. There are two on-deck circles—one for each team.

Outfield: That part of the field beyond the **infield**. Also, the positions played by three players: the right fielder, the center fielder, and the left fielder.

Pop-Up: A batted ball that is hit very high and stays in the infield.

Relief Pitcher: A replacement pitcher—a *reliever*—for another pitcher.

Rookie: An athlete in his or her first year of play for a professional team.

Single: The batter arrives safely at first base.

Stand-Up Double/Triple: The batter reaches second base (a double) or third base (a triple) without needing to slide.

The Box: Also called the batter's box, this is the clearly marked area—measuring four feet wide by six feet long—on either side of home plate within which the batter stands. A right-handed batter stands in the box to the right of home plate (from the perspective of the pitcher); and a left-handed batter stands in the box to the left of home plate (again, from the perspective of the pitcher).

Triple: The batter arrives safely at third base.

Saturday, June 21st

The familiar red sign twinkled in the summer sky above me: "Welcome to Haney Field ~ Home of the Harpoons."

Looking up at that lighted sign, I smiled, because tonight I was coming to the stadium as more than just a fan. Tonight, and for the next six days, I was going to be the bat retriever for my favorite minor-league Class A baseball team in my own hometown of New Blackburn, Massachusetts.

The security guard at the entrance to the players' parking lot waved my dad and me right in. *That* was a first. As we walked through the stadium doors, I heard someone calling my name. "April? April O'Day?"

Spinning around, I saw a tall, slim woman with stylishly short brown hair rushing towards us. When she got closer, I said, "Yes, hi, I'm April, and this is my father, Danny."

"Hello, I'm Beth Harrelson, director of promotions for the Harpoons. I'm so happy to meet you both," she said, smiling warmly, talking quickly, and shaking our hands. She was wearing a red-and-white Harpoons jersey with jeans and white sneakers. She reminded me of my mom: pretty and fashionably casual. "Congratulations again on winning our essay contest!"

"Thanks, Ms. Harrelson."

"Oh, please. Call me Beth."

I won this bat-retriever job with an essay about something that even my dad, a former minor-leaguer himself, doesn't completely understand but which I find super easy and fun. It's called sabermetrics, and it's all about baseball records, math, and statistics.

Beth checked her watch. "Well, how about that? We're running ahead of schedule. Let's take a tour first, shall we?" She was already walking away briskly—and expecting us to follow.

"April, that sounds like fun," my dad said. "But do you need me for this?"

"No, I can handle it."

"All right, honey. Remember, I'll be sitting in the front row."

"Okay, I'll find you, Dad." I gave him a quick hug and ran to catch up with Beth.

First, she took me down to the field to watch the players take their practice swings. From there, we went to the bullpen, where the pitchers were warming up. Then, it was on to the dugout!

"And here's *your* spot," she said, guiding me to the second step leading up to the field. Fortunately, there was a sturdy fence between the hitters and me, so I would be protected.

"We have two rules, April. One, you will wear a batter's helmet at all times, okay?" Beth said.

"Sure!" I replied.

"And two, you'll only come onto the field to retrieve the bat once the ball is back in the pitcher's hand, understood?"

"Absolutely." I couldn't stop smiling. This was actually *happening!*

Spreading her arms wide, she added, "You probably don't realize it, but this place has quite a history. Full of ghosts, I like to say."

"Ghosts?" I said. "Really? Cool."

"Well, not *real* ghosts, of course."

"Oh."

"Sorry to disappoint you. No, I meant that this stadium has been home to baseball for *eighty* years. To celebrate, I'm updating our website and collecting photos to tell our story. Would you like to contribute a photo essay about your experience here—you know, "South Coast Fan Finds Fun!"— or something like that?"

"That sounds great. I got a digital camera for my birthday this year, so I'm all set."

We jogged over to Beth's office to pick up my uniform. It was exactly like the ones the players and the coaches wore, except mine didn't have a number.

I kept my cap low with the brim flat, drew my shoulder-length hair into a ponytail, and pulled the red leggings up high, the way baseball players are supposed to wear them. The long part of the "p" in "Harpoons" was actually shaped like one. Neat.

Checking myself in the mirror—I'd even brought eye black to make those stripes under my eyes—I decided that I looked like a genuine player, freckles and all!

I was *ready!*

* * *

Our opponent that night was the Springfield Braves, the *worst* team in the league. I retrieved the bats without any problems. As promised, Beth stopped by every so often to see how I was doing. I was having a ball! The players spat and scratched themselves (lovely), but they also said nice things to me, like, "Good job!"

After six innings of outstanding bat retrieval, I figured it was time to make myself a little more useful to the team. I had been keeping track of each player's bat size. Although most players had chosen the correct bat for themselves during batting practice, I could tell by the way some of them were swinging that they *really* needed my help.

A new left fielder named Juan Santiago was one of them. He had recently joined the team—a rookie, like so many of the others. I'd watched him hit plenty of times and had gotten a good look as he swung his huge 34-ounce bat. Sure, he could hit some pitches out with that size, but his swing never seemed quite right from *my* vantage point.

In the bottom of the seventh inning, he was standing near me while fastening his batting gloves, waiting for his turn. I went to the rack and chose a lighter bat.

"That's not my bat," he said, with a gentle smile. He was a tall kid, but not exactly beefy. "I use the thirty-four."

"This pitcher's hitting ninety-five today," I said, meaning the miles per hour of his fastball. "This is the bat for you: Thirty-two inches and thirty-one ounces of pure hitting perfection. Tony Gwynn hit almost four hundred with this size."

He took it and held it out, checking the weight. "But I want to hit like Albert Pujols. I need some thunder." He made a weak attempt at flexing.

"Pujols mostly uses a thirty-one ounce bat." I crossed my arms and gave him my best serious look.

He squinted at me. "Really?"

"Really." I may know the Harpoons' stats, but I know the major-leaguers' even better.

"How old are you, Blondie?"

"Twelve. And my name is April."

He tried to stare me down but failed. Finally, he shook his head and re-gripped the bat. "Well, April, speaking of twelve, I'm oh-for-twelve using thunder bat since I got here, so why not?"

He walked up the stairs with the lighter bat, took some warm-up swings in the on-deck circle, and then headed to the plate. On the third pitch, he laced a clean double down the third-base line to put the team up by four runs. When the next hitter singled, Juan scored, knocking the pitcher out of the game.

During the pitching change, Juan came over to see me.

"How do you know so much about baseball?"

I kept my eyes on the new pitcher. "My dad's a former minor-leaguer and he's taught me a lot. Plus, I read tons of baseball books. I check the scouting reports. Stuff like that. I've been around."

"You've been around, huh? A whole twelve years." He laughed. "I got a pair of cleats older than you."

"Don't believe me? Ask me anything about baseball."

"Okay. What award is given to the best pitcher in each league?"

"Cy Young Award," I said. Too easy.

"How about this one: How many consecutive games did Cal Ripken play?"

"That would be 2,131. He broke Lou Gehrig's record from 1939. But those are *trivia* questions, Juan. Ask me about the game. You know, what happens on the field."

He removed his cap and ran his fingers through his short hair. "Okay, let's say next time I'm up, I see the third baseman playing back a few feet. Do I lay down a bunt?"

"Nope. Bad idea."

"Why? Bunting is one of my specialties."

I turned and looked him straight in the eye. "It's a trap, Juan. The third baseman will back up a step to get you to bunt. Earlier in the game, it would have been smart. But this reliever is the best fielding pitcher in the league, and he covers twice the ground of most pitchers. His range factor and total zone runs are out of this world. At the beginning of the season, you may have beaten it out, but that ankle injury you suffered last week has cost you a step."

"Wow, Blondie, that's amazing."

"It's April. And my advice is to use the thirty-one ounce and let 'er rip."

He smiled, balled his right hand, and put it out. It was my first fist bump of the season.

Saturday, June 28th – Wednesday, July 2nd

After a few more games, the players got used to having me around and offering advice. My one-week stint was over way too fast. When it was time for me to leave, I tried not to cry ('cause as everyone knows, there's no crying in baseball). I said goodbye to as many players as I could. There were more fist bumps than I could count.

Beth walked me down the tunnel after the last game. "So how did you like your experience with the Harpoons?" she asked.

"Oh, it was a *total* blast! I can't tell you how much I'm going to miss being in uniform and hanging with these guys."

"Well, you can keep the uniform, April. And you know what? Some of the players and coaches are going to miss you, too. In fact, several have asked me if you can stay on through the summer. I'll have to run it by the owner, but I can't imagine he'll have an issue with it. The team comes back from their road trip in a couple of days. What do you say?"

I tried to appear calm, but inside I was jumping up and down like a maniac.

"Okay, thanks! I'll have to ask my parents," I said, trying to act casual, "but I'm positive they'll say yes."

I was overjoyed—and would have done a cartwheel . . . if I knew how.

* * *

Four days later, I was back at my regular spot, retrieving bats and giving advice. I fist-bumped Carl "Cannon" Caswell, the first baseman, as he returned to the dugout. Cannon was an excellent fielder and a power hitter, but as slow as a turtle. Earlier in the game, I had pulled out my trusty stopwatch and timed him going from home to first base in 5.1 seconds! That was a full second slower than most of the other players.

"What's the word on this pitcher, April?" he asked, as he loaded his bat handle with pine tar from a towel. He knew I had been charting the pitches in my head for a while. It was another one of my talents.

"He'll pitch inside with the two-seamer early in the count to make you swing," I said. "Don't. If you're patient, he'll hang a breaking ball." I pointed a finger in his direction. "Money." That meant I was sure.

Cannon laughed as he twirled the bat above his head. "I hope you're right, April."

He waited for his pitch and hammered the curve ball into the right-field seats. As he loped around the bases, I retrieved his bat and met him about halfway between the dugout and home plate.

"Money!" he said, giving me another fist bump.

*   *   *

Many of the players on the Harpoons were guys straight out of high school or college in their first or second year of professional ball—and quite a few of them had never been away from home before, so I considered it my job to help them as much as I could. Some, like Cannon, caught on early. Others were a bit slow.

Roscoe Barnwell, the Harpoons' speedy center fielder who had joined the team the previous game, waited on the steps next to me a few innings later. I'd been watching the lefty relief pitcher closely, tracking his move to first base to pick off any runner who dared to venture too far. I looked over at Roscoe. "Watch the pitcher's hands," I said.

"What?" He put his hands flat against his chest. "Are you talking to me?"

"Yep. Watch his move to first, Roscoe. His hands come up high when he throws to first base, but they're low when he throws to the catcher. It's not much, but it's there."

He gave me a good stare down. "You're the bat girl, right? I'm getting advice from the bat girl?"

"Bat retriever," I replied.

"You should listen to her," Cannon said from behind us. "April knows her stuff."

The batter struck out and Roscoe moved up to the on-deck circle, laughing loudly. "Base-stealing advice from the bat girl. Now I've heard it all."

After the next batter grounded out, Roscoe got up and hit a clean single to left. The pitcher threw over to first base a few times, lifting his hands just like I'd said, and then went to the plate. Roscoe took off on the next pitch and cleanly stole second base. He stood up, dusted himself off, and pointed to the dugout with both hands.

"Money," Cannon said.

The estimated crowd of 2,500 seemed to agree as they cheered loudly.

Money, indeed.

3

After every game, it was my job to put away the bat weights and the pine tar rags and gather the broken bats from both dugouts and dispose of them. Usually, there were six or seven from each team, but tonight's game featured a couple of hard-throwing pitchers who chewed up batters with inside stuff. Twenty bats turned into firewood in the 2-1 win for the Harpoons.

There was a dumpster behind the stadium where the cleanup crew threw most of their trash. It smelled horrible. As I approached with a can full of busted bats, I noticed that the area was nearly overflowing with black trash bags, but I found an opening and let the bats fly.

After the second trip, I decided to return a different way— by going under the bleachers on the first-base side. The sign read EMPLOYEES ONLY, but I figured I was an employee. And anyway, I wanted to see all the ins and outs of the place.

It was fairly dark down there—even with the security lights on—and grungy. Old grounds crew equipment had been pushed into every nook and cranny. And based on the dust and the rust covering the tractors, drags, and rakes, it looked like everything had been there for a while.

Along the wall was something big and rectangular. It was covered in a green tarp, tucked under the grandstands as far as it could go. It seemed out of place, so I went in for a closer look.

When my eyes adjusted to the light, I realized that the mystery item was bigger than I'd originally thought—probably fifty feet long and twenty feet high. Most of it was blocked by large equipment, but a section of it on the left was practically wide open.

Naturally, I was curious. But when I picked up the bottom of the tarp for a peek underneath, a sudden breeze blew it right up into my hand, ruffling it along the length of the enormous object. Then the tarp went flat. *How did a breeze get under here?* Thankfully, it disappeared as quickly as it came. When I started to lift the tarp again, voices interrupted me. A couple of grounds crew guys were heading my way, so I scurried back to the field and made a mental note to check it out again very soon.

*   *   *

The field lights were still blazing at half past eight while I finished packing up in the dugout. When they began to click off, I knew it was time to go. Just as I lifted my backpack, I saw, out of the corner of my eye, what looked like a shadowy essence running from first to second base—and then another on the pitcher's mound. I closed my eyes and shook my head. When I reopened them, I blinked twice to readjust my eyes to the darkness. The shadows had vanished. Weird. I immediately flashed back to Beth's comment about ghosts. I knew she was merely using a figure of speech . . . but then, why was I shivering?

4

Wednesday, July 2nd (Evening)

Dad picked me up right on schedule. In the car, I grabbed a bottle of water from my pack and drank, and drank, and drank. I figured that dehydration must have set in. What else could account for what I had just seen? When my dad questioned me about my level of thirst, I told him I'd explain as soon as I'd checked my messages.

I turned on my phone and saw that I had two of them. I'd had to leave my cell phone off in the dugout because the Harpoons have a strict no-phone policy.

stats?

It was Darren Plummer, my best friend. He'd sent the same text twice, the second one in all caps. He wanted to go over the statistics of tonight's game.

Fortunately for him, it was Dad's part of the week (my parents are separated and have a joint-custody arrangement) and we were heading home with some carryout for a late dinner, so I told Darren to come over. To avoid having to talk about my "water" issue, I chatted about the game the whole ride home.

Darren was waiting for us at the front door. He's short, like me, but cute in his own way. He rode his bike over—he lives only two blocks away—and always wears a helmet. When he takes it off, the consequences of safe biking are evident: His floppy brown hair sticks out in, like, twenty-seven different directions. No amount of coaxing or patting or combing helps, so I think he's stopped trying.

"Tell me everything," he said, as we treated ourselves to

some popcorn and root beer after dinner. "Who did what?"

Dad had already headed into the den to watch his 52-inch high-def TV. We settled for the 42-inch set in the living room.

"It was a complete nightmare," I said. "Missed signs. Missed cutoffs. And don't get me started on the base-running blunders." I was flustered and took a quick sip of root beer to calm down.

Darren grabbed a handful of popcorn, shoved it in his mouth, and then polished off half his root beer. I knew what was coming next and his loud belch proved me right. He sat on the edge of the couch and excused himself with a small smile. At least he was polite.

"April, there are lots of rookies on this team," he said. "That's why they're in New Blackburn—to learn, remember?" He drained the rest of the soda can but without any further aftershocks. "Anyway, let's talk stats."

I went through the game inning by inning, recalling the major plays for him. I didn't need a scorebook; I just have a knack for remembering details like that. He sat back and absorbed it all, gazing contentedly at the real game that was playing on TV.

"I love this TV," he said during a commercial. "High-def rocks. Your dad's landscaping business must be doing well."

"Ha!" I didn't mean to say it, but it slipped out.

"What? You're *lucky*," he continued between fistfuls of popcorn. "He volunteers at school *all* the time. I don't think my dad has ever set foot in our school, except on Parents' Night."

I thought hard about what I was going to say next. Darren was my closest friend, and I figured I owed him the truth. "Okay, you can't repeat what I'm going to tell you to anyone. Ever. Promise?"

"Sure."

The reason my dad is able to volunteer is because he doesn't actually have a landscaping business, or any other kind of business. He got into a very bad car crash when I was seven. Doctors told him he'd walk again, but his back was such a mess, they thought that he'd eventually end up in a wheelchair." I let that statement fill the air along with the smell of popcorn.

"Whoa, April. For real?"

"Yep. It qualifies him for full-time disability, so the government sends him a check every month. His legs and back got better, but he never returned to his real job. I know he still gets the checks, because I saw one on the kitchen counter the other day."

Darren cocked his head to the side. "But he has his own truck with a sign and all the equipment."

"He *tells* everyone he's a landscaper, but he mows only a lawn or two a week. He can come to school because he has nothing else to do except cash the stupid checks. I'm pretty sure that's the reason he and my mom separated. But he doesn't know that I know." That last statement stung my throat. "Every morning, before I open my eyes, I say their names—Debby and Danny O'Day. They even *sound* like they belong together, don't you think? I picture them in the kitchen, having coffee and laughing. But then, when I go down to breakfast, it's just me and Mom or just me and Dad. Still think I'm *lucky?*"

Darren lifted the can to his mouth but then realized it was empty. "Wow, April. That's some secret. I . . . I had no idea. Sometimes I wish I had a family secret to share, but my parents are so boring, it's almost painful."

"Oh, then you're not going to like what I have to tell you next."

"What is it?"

"I have *another* secret."

"You're kidding," Darren said.

"Nope."

"Well, don't leave me hanging here. Tell me!"

I moved forward onto the edge of my seat, and he leaned in towards me. "It's about the stadium."

"How can a *building* have a secret?"

"I went under it today and there's something very long and tall leaning against the wall. It's covered with a tarp and it's truly ominous-looking."

"Whoa. That is totally and completely not fair that you get to see it and I don't." He sat back and gave me a reassuring nod. "But that's really cool, April."

I considered telling him about the out-of-nowhere breeze and the bizarre shadows I'd seen from the dugout when the field lights went out, but he might have thought I was crazy. And I sort of doubted it all actually happened, anyway.

Sort of.

Thursday, July 3rd – Friday, July 4th

I have to admit that it felt really good when Roscoe Barnwell and Juan Santiago—both exceptional players with raw talent and astonishing speed—started following my advice. At the next game, Juan, who was using that lighter bat, hit an incredible three-for-four (that's .750!). And Roscoe stole second base twice and turned two singles into doubles and one double into a triple. These two would probably be moving up to Double-A ball before the end of the summer.

Cannon Caswell was all in, all the time. In the dugout after the game, we compared the scouting reports he'd gotten from his coaching staff with my own. (I get most of my information from several online sites. Some might find it extremely boring, but I love it.) I knew I couldn't make our first baseman faster, so I tried my best to make him smarter, baseball-wise.

The next day, we must have become distracted or something, because late in the game against the Montpelier Mountaineers, we started falling to pieces. Easy pop-ups were being dropped and runners were advancing left and right. We were just lucky to make it to the ninth ahead by one run. Except for Cannon, we looked *ridiculous* out there!

At the top of the inning, with two outs, the Mountaineers loaded the bases. Cannon was at first, and he edged towards the first-base line as the best hitter for the Mountaineers came to bat. Earlier in the game, he'd hit two line shots past the second baseman against one of our best pitchers. Yet our manager, Don Smiley, motioned Cannon to move over towards second base.

What on earth was he thinking?! We had a new pitcher in there, and he was a soft thrower who changed speeds a lot. It was clearly time to play the line. I stood on the top step, got Cannon's attention, and waved him to his left. He nodded and moved back over towards first base a few steps.

"Hey," said Smiley, "could you let me do my job?" He waved Cannon back towards second base.

"Okay, Skip," I said, calling him a nickname that managers often get in baseball. "But the batter's a pull hitter." I looked over and saw that Cannon was standing with his hands in a "now what?" position. I tried to nudge him over to the line, but the pitcher went into a windup.

Ben Meeks, one of the coaches, had his notebook open and showed something to Smiley. A scouting report, no doubt.

"Hey, Cannon!" Smiley yelled as he motioned with his hands. "Play the line!"

My eyes were on the game and I didn't say a word, but I knew Smiley was staring at me. Meanwhile, Cannon moved to within a few feet of the chalk. On the next pitch, the cleanup hitter smacked a shot right down the first-base line. Cannon leaped into the air as high as he could and snagged it cleanly to end the inning—and win the game.

"Money," I said, to no one in particular.

*   *   *

I knew he'd take the longest, but Smiley was finally warming up to me. We started talking baseball a little bit before each game. He was a former major-league second baseman with an unremarkable career, but he had the makings of a genuinely successful manager. He knew his players, but not as well as I did. Of course, I couldn't tell *him* that.

"Portsmouth's coming into town tomorrow," he said, as we watched batting practice. "They swept the last two series from us. Their leadoff hitter hammers us every time." He took off his hat and wiped his brow with his sleeve. "They have too much speed, April. Sure wish I could slow them down."

"Maybe we can," I said, removing a paper from my back pocket. It was a plan for how to slow down speedy players by adding sand to the base paths and softening the infield grass.

I held it up in the air and he snatched it. He whipped out a pair of reading glasses, scanned it quickly, and laughed. "You are a piece of work, Miss O'Day. Haney would have my head if we tried something like this." He chuckled as he handed the paper back to me. "We'll have to find another way."

"I figured you'd say that." I had a second piece of paper with me and I took it out of my other pocket. "So . . . let's talk about defense and pitching."

Saturday, July 5th

The Harpoons were in the middle of a doubleheader. With some time on my hands between games, I wandered beneath the grandstands to have another look under that tarp. I tried to lift the corner, but it was tucked pretty well. Someone must have secured it recently. My hard knock-knock-knock on the object underneath gave off a dull thud.

Suddenly, I felt a chill. The large sliding door to the storage area slammed shut, leaving me in almost complete darkness. When something—or someone—passed in front of me, I froze. *What was going on here!* I desperately wanted to run, but my legs wouldn't cooperate. My heart was pounding.

A shadowy figure walked past me, pushing something that appeared to be heavy. *A wheelbarrow?* Focusing as best I could, I saw other images of people. *How?*

Just then, the sliding door opened with a series of squeaks, and light returned to the storage area.

"April?"

I turned to see Joe Clemmons, the husky head grounds-keeper. *Whew!* He was driving a golf cart, pulling a small trailer. Boy, was I glad to see *him!*

"You shouldn't be down here," he said. "Lots of machinery and golf carts come through here. It could be dangerous."

He could say *that* again. My heart was only now returning to its normal rhythm.

"Sorry," I managed to say. "I was heading back from the dumpsters and wanted to explore a little." He didn't seem mad, thankfully. "Um, Joe? What's under this tarp? It's gigantic." I didn't dare mention what I had seen in the dark—as if he would have believed me, anyway.

Joe jumped off the cart and came over. "*That* is the owner's pride and joy. It's an old scoreboard. Mr. Haney told me a few years ago that he hopes to display it again when he expands the stadium. Sounds like he wants to go retro. We have strict orders to leave it here, which is not a problem because this is the only place it'll fit."

"Wow, I've never seen an old scoreboard up close before."

"She's a real beauty."

"I'll bet. I've seen them in black-and-white photos, sure, but not in person."

"Okay, okay, I get the hint. Tell you what, April. After the next game, I'll show it to you, all right?"

"Thanks. That'll be super, Joe!"

"Now, let's get going."

I hopped onto his cart and he drove me near the entrance to the tunnel. I had some pitching strategy to discuss with Smiley. Besides, it would be good to be out in the sunshine again. Darkness and this ballpark were definitely not a good combination for me.

* * *

After the second game, the grounds crew jogged out to rake and repair the field. When they were finished, they dragged the tarp over the infield and wandered off. It was time to meet Joe!

"The scoreboard has always been here," he said loudly, as he closed the large door that led to the storage area under the bleacher seats. He flipped a switch to a bank of dim lights that cast a curious glow on the vinyl cover. I felt much safer with the lights on and with Joe around.

"As I understand," he continued, "it was conveyed to the Haneys in the 1950s, along with the stadium. They had to promise to retain it into perpetuity. The previous owner was sentimental, I guess."

"Sounds like it. Well, let me help you move these old nets."

"Thanks." Once the space was clear, Joe set up a ladder and climbed to the top. "I'll show you the whole thing another day. Moving out the rest of this rusty equipment on the other side will require a crane. So for now, just a peek, okay?"

"Sure, Joe. I understand."

He let the material slide down, revealing the left half of the scoreboard. I stared at it for a moment, and then touched its cool wooden surface. It was painted dark green, one of my favorite colors. The two teams listed on top were the "Grays" and the "BB's." Beneath those were two more rows, one for the home team, the "Harpoons," and in the Guests' slot, the "Giants."

"I don't get it. Four rows? Why?"

"I know," Joe nodded. "It's different, right? The story goes that the former owners created a double scoreboard so that no one would ever forget the last game played at their ball-park by members of the Negro Leagues before the outbreak of WWII. Sometime in the mid-1960s, Mr. Haney replaced that unusual scoreboard—with the four teams' names—with a conventional one with just two rows: one for the home team and the other for the guests. Since then, it's been updated, oh, about two or three more times, to the digital version we have today."

"That's awesome, honoring the Negro Leagues like that. I've heard of the Grays. But who were the BB's?"

"Sorry, April. I've never figured that out," Joe said, as he climbed back up the ladder to reposition the tarp. Just as he was about to cover the scoreboard completely, I noticed a small etched-in design, like a round stamp, on the side.

"What's that, Joe?" I asked, pointing.

"Oh, I believe that's the sign manufacturer's logo—Daisy Signs."

"Cool. The daisy's my birth flower. I was born in April."

"Oh, is that how you got your name?" Joe asked.

"You would think, but no. Opening Day is in April, and my dad's a former player, so . . ."

"Oh, well, that's kinda sweet, too. Listen, we have to wrap this up . . . literally." He laughed. "My work day isn't over yet." He secured the fabric tightly over the corner and climbed down off the ladder.

"Thanks for showing it to me, Joe."

I headed out the door but then peered back at the big green tarp. There was a secret under there. I could just feel it.

Thursday, July 10th

My parents worked out a chauffeuring schedule for my summer at the ballpark. No matter where I was sleeping, they each wanted to spend as much quality time with me as possible, so they split the driving duties in half. Mom drove me to the park on Thursday night.

"I packed your rain gear, April," she said as we approached the stadium. "There's a sixty percent chance of a storm tonight. Those metal seats attract lightning, so please take cover if you hear thunder."

"Okay, but I'll be fine, Mom." I didn't have the heart to tell her that real baseball players, even bat retrievers, don't wear rain gear. Ever. It's an unwritten rule.

"There's another storm coming this weekend," she continued. "I brought an umbrella for you to take to your dad's house."

"Thanks, Mom."

Besides being *slightly* overprotective (she's a bit concerned about my being hit by a baseball and has explained to me, many times, that she loves how my mind works and doesn't want anything to ever hurt my ability to think), Mom has this crazy fear of storms, called astraphobia. It's really ironic, because she works in the meteorology department at our local TV station.

Her anxiety wasn't much of a problem until she and Dad split up. After that, she began keeping the TV on the Weather Channel almost all the time. So that night, the combination of worrying about flying baseballs and possible bad weather almost put her over the top. Fortunately, we arrived at the stadium in one piece.

The storm stayed south as the Harpoons cruised to an easy victory. Beth came to see me after the game. She seemed to be smiling even more than usual.

"The owner of the Harpoons wants to meet you," she said. "I'm impressed, April. You're the first bat retriever who's made it all the way to the top. Come on. I'll show you the way to his box."

As a result of my researching him on the Internet, I knew a lot about Mr. Haney. For instance, he'd made a fortune distributing seafood beginning in the 1970s. From there, he went into the real estate business, selling land, which allowed him to open other businesses, such as a limousine service.

His family had purchased the stadium in the early 1950s, after he graduated from college. At the same time, they bought the Harpoons—a struggling team from New Haven, Connecticut—and brought them to New Blackburn. Then they transformed rickety old Cogburn Stadium into Haney Field. According to the team's website, Walter "had always loved baseball and was thrilled that his family owned the team." He took over as managing owner after his parents retired to Florida in February 1963, six months before his twenty-ninth birthday.

As Beth and I walked to the owner's box, the lights started turning off, one by one, giving the field a spooky appearance. Beth knocked on the door.

"Come in, come in," a voice boomed.

As we entered, Walter Haney—an energetic-looking man with an enthusiastic smile—extended his hand to shake mine firmly and invited us to the front of his box. As expected, it had a perfect view of the field.

"April, Beth tells me you're doing a bang-up job for us!"

Haney's voice sounded much younger than his nearly eighty years.

"Thanks," I said. "I love coming here. I don't think I've missed more than a handful of home games since I was five years old."

"I love it! Our number one fan!" Mr. Haney said.

We chatted for several minutes about the team, and then he turned to Beth.

"Would you excuse us, please? April and I have some things to discuss."

"Certainly. I'll be outside if you need me, Walter."

As the door closed behind her, Mr. Haney gestured to a seat in the front row. "Let's sit here, April. There's something I want to ask you."

Mr. Haney was staring straight ahead into the darkness but said nothing, which was kind of odd since he'd said he wanted to ask me something.

"Okay," he finally said, pointing. "Look out there. What do you see?"

The afterglow from the field lights was nearly gone. All I noticed was the tarp covering the infield. "Not much. The lights are off."

He smiled and stood, and then gestured for me to stand, too. Leaning forward, he swept his hand across the horizon. "Are you sure? Try again."

I stared long and hard without blinking.

All of a sudden, I saw it—a shadowy thing moving on the field, just like the one I had seen before, but a bit more distinct now. I followed the object—it appeared to be circling the bases. Then I saw another one at first base and a third in the outfield. "I do see . . . something!" I said. There was also a shadowy presence on the mound. "Are those players?"

Mr. Haney let out a huge sigh and laughed as he threw

his arms straight up. "Thank God you can see them, April! I thought I was going completely bonkers. I've asked dozens of people. Nobody else has ever seen them. Just you and me, apparently."

"So . . . what are they? Who are they?" Whoever they were, they didn't appear to care that the tarp was over the infield or that it was pitch black down there.

"I'm not entirely sure. They come out at night, when the lights are off and everyone has left the stadium. Well, almost everyone."

I looked over at Mr. Haney as he studied the figures on the field. He appeared to be normal in every way, so it didn't seem like I was dealing with a nut. Besides, if he was crazy, then I was, too.

"Until a minute ago, I thought I was losing my mind," he continued. "Ever since the first week of the season, I've been seeing these, um—"

"Ghosts?" I offered.

"Well, what else can they be?" He folded his arms and watched as if it were the most natural thing to do. So I folded mine, too. The shadowy figures continued to move effortlessly across the field. A knock interrupted us.

"April? Your mother's waiting for you," Beth said through the door.

"Great—thank you. I'll be right there."

Mr. Haney kept his gaze on the field. "What we saw tonight stays in this box. Okay?"

"Sure."

"Now that I know you can see them too, we'll figure out this mystery together. Agreed?"

I thought back to the wheelbarrow and the shadows I saw under the stadium. Those must have been a ghostly grounds crew. "No problem," I told him. "I'll be happy to help you."

34

I just hoped we could make sense of this before somebody carted both of us away for good.

Mr. Haney had a smile on his face as I shook his hand goodnight—and the worry lines across his forehead seemed to relax a little.

Beth and I strode down the ramp to the lower section of the stadium. There was a slight breeze, but the smell of concession food still hung in the air.

"Did you see them, April?" Beth asked, as we waved to a security guard.

I wondered if she had been listening at the door. I decided to play dumb. "See what?"

"It's okay. He asks everyone about the shadows. If we didn't know him better, we'd say Mr. Haney is beginning to lose it."

We came to an opening between sections of the grandstands. The field was visible on my right, and I glimpsed something—or someone—crossing home plate.

"Yeah, crazy," I replied.

Just like me.

Friday, July 11th

Even though I'd promised I wouldn't, I decided I *had* to tell *someone*. I texted Darren a cryptic teaser:

ghost players at night

He texted back:

what?

I figured he would say that, so I sent the final text of the night:

will explain tomorrow
come over after your dentist appt

The next afternoon, Dad was in his den—absorbed in a major-league game—so Darren and I had the living room once again.

"Okay, what's going on?" he asked, as he made himself comfy on our couch. "I spent hours trying to figure out what 'ghost players at night' meant. I'm guessing you ran out of human players to annoy, so you found a whole new team 'on the other side,' as they say?"

"Close!" I grinned. "Amazingly close. And I don't annoy the players. They love me, remember?" I picked out a cashew from the bowl and chucked it at him.

He didn't answer, but he did eat the nut.

I told him about my visit with Walter Haney and what we had witnessed from his box.

"So how is it that you two see them but nobody else can?" he asked. "Ooooh . . . maybe you've joined the undead! Maybe you invited me here as part of your evil plan to steal my soul!" He made a cross with his index fingers. "Back, evil one! Back to your dark and foreboding place!" He hissed at me and moved to the top of the couch, which creaked under the strain.

"Cute. But you better come down before you break the frame. We undead don't take kindly to broken furniture."

Darren scampered down and moved closer. "Okay, back to the ghost players. You're just busting me, right?"

"No, I'm dead serious. I really saw them."

I think he was half expecting me to burst out laughing and say, "Gotcha!" But I didn't even crack a smile.

"You really saw something? Wow. This would freak me out if it weren't you."

"Thanks. But it *is* freaky. I'm not sure what's happening. Why can *I* see them? I don't think I have any special powers, do you?"

"You mean, other than being a baseball geek?"

That cost him two more nuts. "You're not helping."

"Okay, okay. So this Haney guy asks every employee to look at the ghost players, right?"

"Yep. But apparently, until now, no one else could see them. In fact, they've all decided he's crazy. I don't know. Maybe it's an age thing."

"What do you mean?" Darren asked.

"Well, he's almost eighty years old, and I'm twelve. Everyone else he's asked is much older than I am and decades younger than he is. Plus, people who are in the middle have a lot to keep track of. My mom calls it turbulence. Maybe he and I have some extra space in our minds to receive these kinds of signals. I don't know. What do you think?"

"I like it. And so, according to your theory, I should be able to see them, too. But even if your theory is wrong, then I'd like to think I'm as special as you are and will be able to see them anyway."

Special, huh? Well, that sounded nicer than *crazy*.

Darren propped a couple of pillows behind his head and got comfortable. "Now tell me about the real game from last night. You know, the one with the players that you *and* everyone else could see. Then let's figure out when I can get in there and see these ghosts for myself."

We went over last night's game for the next half hour, one baseball geek to another.

Naturally, I couldn't help but fixate on, what I called, the shadow players. The Harpoons were away for a short road trip so my services weren't needed, which gave me plenty of time to think on Saturday. I couldn't wait for Darren to see them. Fortunately, local American Legion teams were often allowed to use the field when the Harpoons were away. I checked the paper the following morning and noticed that there was a game scheduled for that night at six. As my dad didn't have much else to do, I was able to convince him to take me—and Darren, too. Tonight was the night!

We sat up high, directly under the owner's box. I wanted the best view of the shadow players.

When the game ended—it was a short one, a pitchers' duel that finished in less than two hours—I kept Dad occupied with a discussion about which pitcher had a better shot at getting drafted. I didn't care about winning the argument (for once); I merely wanted to stay long enough for the lights to go out.

Darren had a small sketchpad and was drawing various Major League Baseball teams' logos. He could draw all of them from memory.

"Excellent Blue Jay!" I said.

"Thanks. It's from the early nineties. That was a great time to be a Jays fan."

Then the field lights went out.

"Okay, let's go," Dad said, standing up and stretching. "Wait—I need to make a pit stop first. I'll be back to get you in ten minutes."

I was counting on that, as he always consumes a significant amount of water during a game. Darren and I immediately got to work scanning the field.

"What, exactly, should I be seeing?" he asked, as he put his hand above his eyes to shield them from light that wasn't there.

"Just look. You'll either see them or—"

They appeared. One shadow player was clearly leading off first base. "There!" I pointed. "He's on first."

Although Darren was listening to me, he kept his eyes glued to the field.

"Now he's on second!" I said. "He stole it."

"I . . . I don't see anything." He was trying too hard.

"Try relaxing, Darren. It's like the first time you see a Magic Eye 3-D picture: Nothing, nothing, nothing, and then wham! It jumps out at you. Let the entire field enter your vision at once."

He stared for a moment longer; then, slowly, pointing to third base, he moved his finger in tiny circles. He started stammering incoherently, but his smile said it all.

"I know!" I nodded. "He just stole third."

"They're like . . . transparent shadows," he said, finally finding his words. "And . . . and they're everywhere!"

"I wonder who they are," I said. "They're obviously baseball players, but who are they—and why are they at Haney Field?"

"I don't know, April." He grabbed a fistful of popcorn from the bag he'd been holding and began munching away. "We can't be sure what we're dealing with here."

"I'm tempted to run down on the field to try to talk to them. Are you with me, Darren?" I was just busting him, but it was fun to watch him squirm. When I jumped out of my seat, he clutched my arm.

"Are you nuts?" He saw me smile and pushed my arm away in disgust. "Good one, April. Almost had me."

All of a sudden, the bag of popcorn Darren was holding went flying. Popcorn sprayed everywhere and the bag landed in the row behind us.

"What the heck?" Darren examined his empty hands.

I leaned over to pick up the bag and noticed something unusual about it. Or rather, that something unusual was *on* it. It was spherical and translucent, but still visible from the right angle.

"A shadow ball!" I said. "One of theirs!"

I was definitely unprepared for what happened next. As I reached out to touch the ghostly ball, it materialized beneath my fingertips. Then, as I held it, the players suddenly transformed from shadows to real players, playing an actual game in broad daylight. The grass was a vibrant green and the stadium had an old-timey look to it. The signs on the outfield fence were for products I'd never heard of. The players wore baggy uniforms and fielded with tiny gloves. All around me in the bleachers were fans, cheering. I froze.

"April?" I heard Darren say faintly. "Hey, April?"

I shuddered, as if I had eaten a lemon, and dropped the ball. The field plunged back into darkness and I became aware of Darren repeatedly poking me in the arm.

"You okay? You spaced out for a second. Like you weren't there."

As I searched for the ball, Darren continued to poke me in the arm.

"Earth to April!" he said.

I grasped his finger in mid-poke and turned it away. "I'm fine. I'm fine. But I just saw something absolutely incredible."

"What?"

"I saw the players, Darren. When I touched their ball,

the game came to life. The field, the players, the fans, the sunshine, the colors—everything!"

"Cool! Can I see them, too?"

"I dropped the ball. I don't know where it went."

He gave me a "how convenient" look, and a voice interrupted us before he could do any further interrogation.

"Ready to roll, guys?" Dad called from behind us.

"Sure," I said. "But let's clean up first."

Darren retrieved his soda bottle and I picked up his nearly empty popcorn bag. As I bent down, I saw it—the faint outline of the shadow ball underneath one of the seats. I carefully scooped it into the bag without being seen.

"Can I have the rest of this?" I asked Darren, showing him the bag. "I might want a snack later."

"Help yourself."

Tucking the popcorn container with the ball into my backpack, I wondered: Could this be my ticket to shadow land whenever I wanted?

The next morning, I found a small leather pouch to hide the shadow ball in. I opened the popcorn bag and glanced inside. The ball was still there but was now *semi-transparent.* I gently removed it and held it in my palm. Nothing happened. *Oh, no! It must be broken*, I thought. *My ticket to shadow land is gone.*

Then it hit me. Of course it didn't work. I wasn't at the stadium. As far as I knew, there were no shadow players in my neighborhood. They were only at the ballpark. Anyway, I'd find out soon enough—the Harpoons were playing tonight!

* * *

When it was time to go, I slipped the pouch into my pack and, after Dad dropped me off, headed to the dugout.

Once I'd settled in, and when nobody was paying attention, I opened the pouch and peeked inside. The shadow ball was back to its original transparent form. I plopped my backpack in its usual out-of-the-way spot in the corner.

The Harpoons had returned from their road trip, during which they'd lost two out of three games. Roscoe Barnwell and Juan Santiago had both been promoted to the Double-A team earlier than I'd expected, and new faces were arriving every day.

The new left fielder, a big guy named Kyle Bonner, was talking with Cannon at the other end of the dugout just before Kyle's first at-bat. He approached me while putting on his batting gloves. "Hey, bat girl?"

"It's April, and yes, I'm the bat retriever."

Kyle strapped his right glove closed and clapped it loudly.

Cannon said you can pick me out some lumber. So what do ya say?"

I eyed him top to bottom. Having watched him take a few swings in batting practice, I already knew the answer, but I wanted to have some fun. "How tall are you, Kyle? Six four, maybe?"

"Yeah, six three and change."

"Put out your hands, please."

He smiled and put his hands straight out.

"Palms up," I said. "Fingers apart."

He laughed a little, but he did it.

"Go with the S318 maple," I said. "Thirty-three inch, thirty-two ounce. You'll find it in the upper right corner of the bat rack."

"You're sure that's the bat for me?"

"Positive as a proton!" I love it when I can use something from one of my classes in everyday conversation, and Kyle seemed happy with—and only a bit confused by—my answer as he pulled out the bat from the rack. His left hand traced the surface and then he gripped it.

"Feels like a million bucks. Thanks, April."

"You're welcome. And move up in the box. This guy's cutter is sharp tonight."

I wondered about some of these players. They seemed so full of talent and determination, yet they lacked some basic insights into the game. It's actually not that hard.

Cannon was at the plate, and he fouled off pitch after pitch. Kyle spat sunflower shells onto the steps and leaned in my direction.

"April, why's he called Cannon? He sure doesn't look like one."

I had the answer down pat. "He was a pitching prospect out of high school. Used to have an arm like a cannon," I said. "But after two arm surgeries, he couldn't pitch anymore, so he came back as a first baseman. Now he has a weak arm, but at least he can hit the ball hard." *Crack!* As if we'd had it all planned, Cannon lined the next pitch over the right-field wall. "See? Like it was shot from a cannon."

Kyle was a little anxious his first time at bat and popped up to end the inning. He never blamed the bat, though, and eventually went two-for-four in the game. Not bad for a rookie.

I stayed as long as I could afterwards, slowly walking behind the stadium to toss the broken bats into the dumpster. I even volunteered to help sweep the dugout, but a field worker wouldn't let me. I strategically left my pack in the corner.

As the field lights went out, I met Beth at our usual spot so she could escort me to the parking lot. She talked a mile a minute while we walked.

"My backpack!" I yelled, stopping abruptly and nearly causing her to bump into me. "I left it in the dugout!"

"Oh, no problem. I'll call security for you." She started dialing her phone.

"That's okay. I can get it. It'll only take a minute."

"But April, please let me—"

"I'll be quick!" I was gone before she could stop me.

Back in the dugout, I grabbed my pack from its hiding place and pulled out the leather pouch. I took a deep breath as I turned it upside down. The shadow ball dropped into my hand.

In an instant, I was at the shadow game. The field had been dark a second ago, but now it was bursting with activity, and the sun shone brightly from the right-field sky. As my eyes adjusted to the scene, I realized something about the players that I hadn't noticed before: They were all African

American. So were the umpires, the coaches, and everyone in the stands. This was obviously a game from the Negro Leagues, back when baseball was a segregated sport. From the fans' clothing, I guessed it was sometime around 1940. (When my mom isn't worrying about the weather, she likes to watch classic movies—and she insists that I join her. I have to admit it: hot chocolate and Jimmy Stewart are not a bad combination.)

And another thing stood out: the team name emblazoned on the uniforms. These were the Blue Barons. That must have been the 'BB's' on the old scoreboard! I tried to take in as much as I could, but there was so much going on. I squinted to see the right fielder make a great running catch while heading towards the bleacher seats down the first-base line.

The inning ended and the Blue Barons came off the field and into the dugout. Nobody seemed to notice me, or maybe they were simply ignoring me. Was I visible or not? I really wanted to stay, but I knew I had to go because Beth was waiting, so I dropped the shadow ball back into its leather pouch.

Instantly, darkness returned and I was alone in the Harpoons' dugout. I placed the pouch inside my pack and ran out of there as fast as I could. Beth was tapping her foot when I caught up with her, and I saw my dad's truck parked nearby.

*   *   *

Now that I knew the team's name, I couldn't wait to get going on my investigation. I did a full Internet search that night for the Blue Barons and discovered the Barons, the Black Barons, and the Blue Birds—but no Blue Barons. I checked every site I knew (and I know a lot of them) but found nothing. I even flipped through some old baseball reference books. None of them mentioned the Blue Barons.

This was *completely* unacceptable. *Everything* about baseball has been recorded, even box scores from games in the 1870s. Who were the Blue Barons? I had to know.

It was going to take another visit to their game to gather the information we needed. But it occurred to me that it probably wasn't a good idea to be in the Blue Barons' dugout. I couldn't tell if anyone could see me, but since I would stick out prominently in a Negro League crowd, I figured it would be best to stay under the bleachers and out of the way.

My chance came after the next game.

* * *

Tuesday, July 15th

The lights went off as I was returning from the dumpster with the broken bats. I ran to the dugout and grabbed my shadow ball—and my digital camera, too. Immediately, the stands above me were filled with cheering fans. I moved to a section under the bleacher seats, down the right-field line. The bleachers were made of wood and the whole thing creaked and swayed. Moving closer to the field, I stuck the shadow ball into the back pocket of my uniform—and it worked! I was still at the shadow game, but now I had both hands free.

There was a lot of daylight streaming in between two boards several feet ahead. I peeked through and got an excellent view of the field and, more specifically, the right fielder. He was thin and wiry, but from what I'd read, many of the players were like that in those days. He made a running catch right in front of me. I took six or so pictures of him—just in time.

"Nice catch, Flash!" someone yelled.

The right fielder tipped his cap to the crowd and then ran to the infield. The inning was over. The sound of stomping feet above me was deafening, but I stood my ground with my hands over my ears to absorb as much as I could of the scene. The opposing team, the Grays, took the field, and I watched as the pitcher warmed up. The first two batters struck out.

"Now batting," boomed the announcer, "right fielder, Flash Henderson."

The crowd cheered wildly as he dug in. He took a pitch and then laid a perfect bunt down the third-base line. He was past first before the third baseman could even make a play. No wonder they called him Flash. He had to be the fastest runner I'd ever seen. He reminded me of the speedy shadow I saw that night in the dugout after the game. When the next batter launched a home run over the left-field fence, Flash scored. Next time, I was *definitely* going to find out just how quick he really was.

I wanted to see more, but it was time to go back. I placed the shadow ball in its pouch, and the field was dark once again, with only a few lights on for security. Before putting my camera away, I glanced quickly at the screen to look at the first photo I'd taken. But it was blank. As I scrolled through the shots, I noticed that all of them were empty black rectangles. Weird.

I dropped the camera into my pack and ran to meet Beth at our usual spot so she could walk me to Dad's truck. She never knew I'd been gone.

*   *   *

When I returned home, I took some more photos to see if my camera was broken. Nope. It was perfect. Sadly, though, I had no evidence of shadow land.

Well, at least I had something else to go on now: the name Flash Henderson. I'd never heard of anyone named Flash and assumed it was a nickname. *No mother would name her son that, would she?*

After breakfast, I got down to work reading about players from seventy-five years ago, but there was nothing about Flash in the record books. Who was he?

Later that afternoon, Darren appeared at my door.

"Don't you answer your phone anymore? I've called all the hospitals looking for you," he said, out of breath. "I honestly thought this was the end of April O'Day." He squared his shoulders and folded his arms. "I had youse dead and buried." This was such a good imitation of his mother that I had to smile.

When he told me he'd been trying to reach me, I checked my phone and plugged it in. "Sorry, drama king. My phone ran out of juice. Anyway, listen. I think I'm onto something."

"What?"

"Not what. Who. Flash Henderson."

"Who's that?" he said, quickly nabbing his spot on the couch.

"A shadow player. I've seen the game in daylight twice now—once from the dugout and another time from under the bleachers. Well, sort of in daylight. It's like a flashback or something. Henderson is the right fielder and the only player whose name I know. But I can't find any intel on him—*or* his team!"

Darren sat straight up. Usually, he was relaxed—too relaxed, even—but now he seemed uptight.

"How did you see them?" he asked, trying to smooth down a tuft of hair above his left ear.

I reached for my leather pouch and sat beside him. "Remember that shadow ball that hit your popcorn bag at the Legion game? Well, I found it before we left." I took his hand and plopped the semi-transparent ball into it. "Holding this after dark at the stadium lets you see their game in full daylight."

With his other hand, Darren felt the smooth surface of the ball.

"You didn't by any chance remember to bring your camera, did you?"

"Umm-hmm."

"Great! Let me see!" Darren said.

I shook my head. "Sorry. I took six pictures and they all came out blank. I guess our technology doesn't work in their time."

"Ugh!"

"I know—it stinks! But guess what I learned. It's a Negro League game between the Blue Barons and the Grays. They just keep playing, Darren, night after night. It's daytime for them when they play, but it's night for us. Doesn't make much sense, does it?"

"Sure it does," he said, "if you know how to speak April-ese. I happen to be fluent in it." He assumed a more relaxed position on the couch. "So, you've been camped out here at Casa O'Day, trying to find information on the Blue Barons and a player named Flash Henderson. Google is no help. Your reference books turn up nothing. You're practically pulling your hair out because you don't have any answers." He placed his hands over his ears. "Say it ain't so, Joe?"

I could have done without the sarcasm, but otherwise he was right on.

"Okay, Mr. Hear No Evil. I'd be really ticked off right now if you weren't so, so—"

"So *right?*"

I needed something to toss at him, but all I had was a throw pillow. He was ready for it and it landed harmlessly on the floor.

"You're going about it all wrong," he said. "Some information simply can't be found with the touch of a button. What we need is an expert—someone who knows all about the Negro Leagues and its history. That's what we need."

Darren was absolutely right. But *who* was that *someone?*

*   *   *

Friday, July 18th

After the next Harpoons game, Beth walked with me to the owner's box before I had a chance to visit the shadow game again. She led me in and then quietly closed the door. Mr. Haney was standing in the front of the box staring out at the dark field.

"Everyone thinks the lights go off thirty minutes after the game because it's a city ordinance or something," he said. "Truth is, *I* made the rule." He pointed to the field. "I did it for *them.*"

The shadow players used to be hard to see, but now I could make out the entire game.

"So April, you've had an interesting week, haven't you?"

"What do you mean?"

"The advantage of this box is its view. I can see all the comings and goings on the field . . . and in the dugout, too. You have something to tell me, don't you?"

"You're right, Mr. Haney. I do."

I knew it! Mr. Haney exclaimed.

"These past few days have been strange . . . and wonderful. First of all—"

There was a knock on the door. Beth poked her head in. "Excuse me, Mr. Haney. Mrs. Haney is on the line, and she says that if you aren't home soon, she can't guarantee that you'll enjoy dinner tonight."

"Thank you, Beth. Well, that's my cue, April. I'm sorry to have to cut our meeting short. But I have an idea! I'd like to invite you and your parents to my home for dinner tomorrow evening. The team is in New York, so my slate is clean. What do you say? You can fill me in then."

It sounded like fun, except for the "parents" part. "My parents are separated. But I'm sure my dad would love to come. It'll be his Saturday night with me."

"Outstanding. I'll send a driver to your house at six o'clock."

I decided to push my luck. "Is it okay if I invite my friend Darren? He can see the shadow players, too."

Without hesitating, he said, "Of course, April. Darren is more than welcome. See you tomorrow."

*   *   *

Darren was waiting by our front door when we pulled into the driveway. After Dad disappeared into the den, I said, "Try not to act like a complete dork, okay?" That's how I broke the news to him about Mr. Haney's invitation.

"Aw, c'mon, April! I'll do my deranged umpire impression. It'll be a hoot!"

"Don't even *think* about it."

"I can give signs like a real third-base coach." He went through a series of them, touching various parts of his body in rapid succession. He was impressive, but still.

"Darren, this is an important get-together, not an audition.

He wants to discuss the shadow players. Why else would he want us to come over?"

"That's easy. To hear my announcer impressions."

Darren was such a nut . . . but he was all I had.

* * *

My next trick was breaking the news to Dad. Some days, he loved the idea of doing something different; other days, not so much.

"We've been invited to dinner tomorrow by Mr. Haney, the owner of the Harpoons," I said to my dad, who was relaxing in his favorite chair with a new novel (like me, he loves a good whodunit). "Isn't that great? He's even sending a limo. I've never been in one before."

"Why is he inviting us, April? After all, we're not exactly in his *league* . . . pun intended."

"Good one, Dad. Listen, he's not like that. Mr. Haney doesn't live in a mansion or anything, and he drives himself to the stadium every day. I've seen his car. It's a Chevrolet."

"Then what's with the limo?"

"He owns a limo service. He's just trying to be *friendly*, Dad. That's all."

He was silent for a few seconds. "So you really want to go?"

"Yes, I really do. And Darren's invited, too."

"What's the dress code?"

"Strictly casual," I grinned. "Normal clothes will be fine."

He smiled at me, took my hand, and said, "Okay, honey. Looks like we're moving up in the world."

* * *

Saturday, July 19th

The big white limo rolled in front of our house at six o'clock on Saturday evening. My dad actually looked

53

handsome in his striped button-down shirt, tan slacks, and loafers. I'd helped him choose an outfit that coordinated with what I was wearing. While Dad and I were quite a pair, Darren was . . . well, he was a complete surprise. He wore a blue-checked shirt, with rolled-up sleeves, khakis, and a pair of clean sneakers. Score a point for him.

The driver, a Portuguese man named Manny, introduced himself and opened the door of the limo. It seemed like there was more room inside the car than in my own bedroom.

"Awesome," Darren said, as he watched the movie playing on the flat-screen TV.

My thought exactly.

The ride was so smooth that I could barely tell we were moving. Dad stared out the window with a neutral look.

"We'll be there in twenty minutes," Manny said.

I leaned back and enjoyed my first-ever limo ride.

Saturday, July 19ᵗʰ (Evening)

Manny pulled into the circular driveway and opened the car door for us. Walter Haney lived in a cheery Colonial home, with multicolored flowers lining the stone path to the front door.

"Hello!" Mr. Haney said, as he welcomed us inside.

I introduced him to my dad and then Darren, who managed not to say or do anything silly as he shook hands. Darren was really racking up points.

"I hardly recognized you, April," Mr. Haney laughed. "No cap, no uniform, no eye black. You know, I don't believe I've ever seen your eyes before. They're green—like mine!" He turned to my dad. "She's a terrific young lady, Danny."

"Thank you," Dad said. "I think so, too."

Darren smirked and was about to say something, but I shot him my best "don't you dare" expression.

Mr. Haney offered us a tour of the house, chatting with my dad as we walked. We wound up on a large deck overlooking the ocean.

"It's just my wife, Peg, and me now. When the kids left the nest many years back, we bought this place and we couldn't be happier. We didn't want a lot of unused rooms."

"Is Mrs. Haney here?" I asked.

"No, I'm sorry to say. At the last minute, she was recruited to babysit our great-grandkids. But I'd love for you to meet her. Next time."

There were no butlers or maids or chefs, as far as I could tell. Mr. Haney put on an apron and expertly prepared the grill. Obviously, he'd done this many times before.

While Mr. Haney and Dad talked, Darren and I checked out the beach. A ten-foot seawall kept the ocean away from the backyard, and a concrete staircase led us directly to the shore. Darren did his impressions of various pitchers and their windups while tossing rocks into the surf. He wasn't much of a player himself, but he was a gifted mimic.

Mr. Haney served us fish with sweet potato wedges, green beans, and a salad. The iced sun tea was delicious.

After dinner, Dad went for a walk—and to make a call, which he did every night. Very mysterious. Unless, of course, he's calling my mom. Always my secret hope. The rest of us sat on the seawall, drinking more iced tea and preparing for some serious baseball talk.

"So," Mr. Haney began, "let's pick up where we left off last night. You have news, right, April?"

"Yes, and I have something to show you." I reached into my fanny pack and pulled out the leather pouch. "I found one of their game balls. It landed near Darren and me after the Legion game the other night. If I hold onto it, it takes me back to the real game. It's incredible, Mr. Haney. And what I learned was that the players are from the Negro Leagues."

"Ah, that's very helpful," he said, holding his gaze on a group of seagulls flying overhead. "But why are they haunting Haney Field?"

"We don't know . . . yet," I said.

"Well, we need to find out as quickly as possible. This is a two-person job, if ever I saw one. Darren, let's get you out onto the field. Starting the next home game, you're the visiting team's bat boy. Interested?"

Darren kicked his feet against the concrete wall. "Sure. But don't I have to try out or win a contest or something?"

"I own the team. If I say you're the bat boy, you're the bat boy. Rank has its privileges."

A moment later, Dad rejoined us. Our conversation was over for now.

We headed back to the deck for dessert. The sun had set, but not before we got to enjoy a sky full of peaches and pinks. Mr. Haney lit a row of tiki torches to shed some light and keep the mosquitoes away. He brought out two pies, an apple and a pumpkin, and we all dug in. Darren had three slices, of course.

Half an hour later, Manny opened the limo's doors and we climbed in for the trip home. For the first five minutes, we listened to the radio, but then Dad turned it off.

"Mr. Haney offered me a job tonight," he said, his hands fidgeting in his lap.

"I thought you *had* a job," Darren said. "Landscaping services." I wanted to smack him for saying that.

Dad kept his head down. "Most of my landscaping work is in the morning, Darren. This would be a driving job, two hours a day, three days a week."

"That's terrific, Dad!" I cut in. "Are you going to drive a limo, like Manny?"

"Yes. The way Walter explained it, there's this elderly gentleman, an old friend of his, who needs a ride on Mondays, Wednesdays, and Fridays. I'll have that regular assignment, and then I'll be on call the rest of the week."

I'd never seen my dad conflicted like this. I knew he wasn't supposed to be working because of his so-called disability, but I guessed he wanted to do something to fill his days. Sounded like being a part-time driver might let him stay on disability.

"When do you start?" Darren asked, chugging a soda from the cooler.

"Very soon," Dad said. "I have to apply for my chauffeur's license, but I should be on the road shortly."

We were all quiet the rest of the way home, but my dad did manage to crack a smile.

Sunday, July 20th

The next day, Darren took his spot in the visitors' dugout. He smiled and pointed my way during the game, and we had a quick chat in the fifth, when the grounds crew ran out to drag the field. Darren was a natural bat retriever.

To give us more time for our investigation, Mr. Haney made arrangements to have us driven home by one of his drivers after the games. On Sunday night, we all got together in the owner's box. We were quiet until the field lights went out.

It was much easier to observe the shadow players now that we'd gotten used to them. They moved around the field gracefully, playing a game only we could enjoy.

"Mr. Haney," I said, pulling the ball out of my pack, "before we check out the shadow game, do you want to have a look?"

I had thought I'd see a sparkle in his eyes, but what I saw instead was fear. Nevertheless, he held the ball. His face froze as he looked out onto the field. I was sure he could see the players now—the Blue Barons and the Grays—and the cheering crowd and the vendors, just as I'd been able to. He watched for a few minutes and then, without saying a word, held the ball upside down. That was my cue to retrieve it. I positioned the pouch under his palm and he let it drop in.

"Thank you. This *is* interesting, April," Mr. Haney said. "It's time for you and Darren to find out more. We need names, dates—anything you can gather. You take the home team dugout, April. And Darren, you can watch from the visitors'."

You don't want to come with us, Mr. Haney?" Darren asked.

"Not tonight, son. But thank you. I'll join you next time. I have some files to review. I've been putting this task off for weeks. When that's done, I'll have a clearer head."

As we left his box, I had the impression that he wasn't telling us the whole truth. Oh, I'm sure he had things to do, but missing an opportunity like this for paperwork didn't make sense—unless that's what being a grown-up is all about: responsibilities.

* * *

While I had my own shadow ball, we needed another one for Darren. Luckily, because we knew what we were hunting for, it didn't take us long to find a perfect specimen in the bleachers.

Before we went to our respective dugouts, we agreed to make the jump together and return at the end of the current inning. When Darren counted to three, I grasped the shadow ball.

Once again, I was immediately at the game. I could see Darren in the other dugout with a surprised expression on his face. I suddenly remembered he hadn't seen any of this up close and in color before. I was glad to have my best friend on this adventure with me.

The manager in my dugout groused and swore and paced, but he never turned in my direction, even when I called him "Pops." Clearly, he couldn't see me.

The right fielder, Flash Henderson, made a remarkable catch to end the inning, and the Blue Barons ran into the dugout as I stood in the corner. The first batter headed to the plate; and the second, to the on-deck circle. Flash grabbed his bat and waited at the top of the stairs.

"We need runners," I overheard the manager say. "Put one down if you have to."

Flash nodded. Pops wanted him to bunt if he had the chance. It seemed like a good strategy to me.

Since I figured no one was aware of my presence, I quietly said, "Go, Flash."

He turned and looked directly at me. "Who are *you?*"

"You—you can see me?" I felt foolish asking because it was obvious he was talking to me. Nobody else was nearby.

"Of course."

"My name's April. I'm a bat retriever."

"A what?"

"A bat girl."

"Oh, I didn't know we had one."

"Oh . . . well, I—um—I won a contest that the Har—" As I glanced down at my uniform to point out the team's name, I thought better of it. "My uncle owns this stadium, and he said that I could visit with your team and do some bat retrieval."

Thankfully, Flash was due to bat next, so he didn't stop to question me further on his way to the on-deck circle. From what I could tell, no one else had heard our conversation.

I pulled out my stopwatch. With one out and a runner on second, Flash laid down a perfect bunt and burst up the first-base line. He covered the 90 feet from home plate to first base in 3.2 seconds! Wow! The third baseman fielding the ball didn't even have a *chance* to make a play. On the next pitch, Flash easily stole second, and the runner at second stole third. When the clean-up hitter launched a shot over the left-field fence, the crowd went wild. Flash circled the bases and then, along with his two teammates, tipped his cap to the fans before returning to the dugout. The person in charge of the scoreboard added three more runs for the Blue Barons.

"Outstanding bunt," I said.

"Thanks, April! I got lucky."

Anyone ever call you anything other than Flash?" It seemed like a good time to ask.

"Just my mama."

"What does *she* call you?"

"Oscar. But when she calls me Oscar Henderson the Third, I know I'm in *big* trouble."

Seemed like moms hadn't changed much in seventy years. "I know the feeling."

When the inning was over, Flash sprinted out to right field.

I could see that Darren had already left as planned, and I was just about to join him when I noticed a telegram on the bench. I took a minute to read it and then dropped the shadow ball into its pouch. Back on the field in the present, Darren was waiting for me with his arms folded.

"You're late," he said.

"I know. But I found out some good stuff."

"Like what?"

"Tell you when we get to Haney's box."

Mr. Haney was eagerly waiting for us. The first thing we did was recite the names we could remember. Darren had three. Mr. Haney quietly wrote them all down.

"What about you, April?" he asked.

"I talked with one of the players."

That got Mr. Haney's attention—and Darren's, too.

"Really?"

"Cool!" said Darren. "Who?"

"The right fielder who made that great catch to end the inning: Oscar Henderson. They call him Flash. And that's not all. I have two *more* names: Lamont Porter and Henry Calloway. Turns out they sent a message explaining their absence from today's game—a death in the family. Lamont's father passed away and the funeral was in the afternoon. I read it in a telegram that the coach received."

"Well, nobody on the other team even *saw* me," Darren said. "I did all of my announcer impressions but didn't get so much as a smile out of any of 'em. I even burped the first line of the national anthem. Nada."

As gross as that sounded, it did prove a point. Flash was obviously different from the others, but none of us knew why.

"What do you think, Mr. Haney?" He didn't answer. He seemed lost in thought. I snuck a peek at his note pad. He hadn't written down even one of the names I'd given him.

"Oscar Henderson," he said softly, as he stared into the blackness of the stadium. "Oscar, Lamont, Henry . . ."

"Mr. Haney?" He ignored me and just kept repeating the names.

Darren looked at me and shrugged. It seemed our meeting was over. As luck would have it, Beth arrived to say that our driver was waiting to take us home.

Friday, July 25th

During the team's road trip, Cannon fell into a terrible slump: 3 for 17 in four games. I approached him before our next home game while he waited for his turn at batting practice.

"I think they're going to bench me, April," he said, as he leaned against the backstop. "I've never been benched in my life." He spat out some sunflower seed shells. "Not even in Little League."

"Can I borrow your phone?" I asked.

"Why? Don't you have your own?" More seeds went flying.

"Mine's not a camera phone."

"Oh, sure. Here you go."

The new rule was that phones were allowed on the field until batting practice was over so that the players could engage with their fans via social media.

It was Cannon's turn in the cage, and I watched as he swung the bat. I snapped some action shots. He hit three weak grounders and then stopped to talk with his hitting coach. Finally, he smashed a ball over the right-field wall. Unfortunately, he popped up the next three. Cannon wasn't usually an emotional player, but he slammed the bat on the ground as he left the cage.

"Maybe I should just retire," he said to me. Apparently, this called for a fresh batch of seeds. He dumped half the bag into his mouth.

"Don't be silly," I said. I held out his phone to show him some of the shots I'd taken. "By any chance, were you injured on the trip?"

"Yeah, twisted my right knee in the first game. But I'm fine now. Why?"

"Your weight transfer is all wrong." I showed him a still shot and a short video. "You're favoring your right leg and then overcompensating for it. You've developed a bad habit. Ever heard of muscle memory?"

"Yeah . . ."

"Well, you need to re-teach your arms and legs how to bat—by repetition. But don't worry. It's nothing a few hundred swings off the tee won't cure."

"A batting tee? I haven't hit off one of those since T-ball!" He didn't seem to know that hitting from a tee was a common rehab drill.

"There's a small batting cage behind the left-field bleachers. I'll meet you there in ten minutes."

He stared at the video for a second and then let another round of shells fly. "Thanks, April."

I brushed the shells from my shoulders. It came with the territory.

After our practice session, Cannon went three-for-four that night, including the go-ahead home run in the bottom of the eighth inning. I greeted him with a fist bump when he returned to the dugout.

"Money," I said.

"Money," he fist-bumped, flexing his arm. "And muscle memory."

*   *   *

Haney was not in his box after the game, so Darren and I decided to explore. There was something I wanted to show him, anyway.

"Where are you taking me?" he asked, as we entered the area below the grandstands.

"You'll see."

This is what they call the *bowels* of the stadium, right? He sniffed loudly. "I can smell why."

Okay, it was a little musty under there. Fortunately, Mr. Exaggeration didn't bother me. I led him over to the green tarp.

"What's this?" he asked.

I lifted the corner. "It's an antique scoreboard. Joe, the groundskeeper, told me it's Haney's pride and joy."

"Why? It's just a scoreboard." Darren grinned at me for a moment and then leaned over and gripped the edge of it. "Okay, I'll take this side and you get the other." Grunting loudly, he pretended he was going to lift the whole thing.

"Cute. Joe says that Haney may want to use it again. But I'm guessing he's happy with his fancy electronic scoreboard. I can't imagine him wanting to put this one up."

Suddenly, we heard footsteps. Beth appeared from the tunnel. "What are you two doing down here?"

"She's showing me the old scoreboard," Darren said. "It's been here for decades, you know."

"I'm aware of that," she snapped. "I'm also aware that you two don't belong down here."

"We went to see Mr. Haney," I said, "but he wasn't in his box."

"That's because he's away on business. He's not due back for another couple of days."

"But—"

"He left me strict instructions that you are both to leave the stadium immediately after the game."

"But we always hang around—" Darren said.

"Well, not anymore. You have fifteen minutes after the final out to be in the parking lot for your ride. His orders."

Darren looked at me. Something strange was going on.

Beth walked us over to the parking lot and to our waiting car, but Manny was not our driver.

"Listen, I'm sorry about this, kids," Beth said in a softer tone. "But if I don't get you on your way home this minute, I'll be fired."

"What happened? Why is Mr. Haney doing this?" I asked.

"I don't know. But he was emphatic about it, that's for sure. Maybe it's for your own safety."

We didn't say much on the ride home. *What was Haney up to?* I wondered. *If he was trying to keep us from finding out something, that was not going to happen.*

* * *

I called my dad to tell him when we were on our way. A homemade meal was waiting for us when we got home (of course, I'd invited Darren), and Dad still had his driving uniform on. He rarely cooked, so I knew this would be interesting, if nothing else.

"It's a casserole," he said, pouring water into our glasses. "I hope you like it!"

Its main ingredients were camouflaged by a gooey layer of cheese. I was starving, so cheese-covered anything was fine with me. Further inspection revealed elbow macaroni and ground beef underneath. Well done, Dad—a fairly foolproof combination. I bet Mom would be impressed. Before they separated, she was always trying to persuade him to help more around the house. Cooking could have been his specialty.

"So, how was your first day of driving?" I asked.

He blew on a forkful. "Rather uneventful. I had only one passenger all day. There's this elderly Asian man," he said. "You remember. I told you about that old friend of Haney's, Mr. Koh. Never got his first name. Anyway, I stopped by his house and talked with his daughter. She handed me a map and said to take him on the prescribed route. I helped him into the back seat, drove him around for a couple of hours, and brought him home. Easiest hundred bucks I've ever made."

is he a friendly person?" Darren asked.

"I'm sure he is, but . . . I don't really know."

"What do you mean, Dad?"

"Well, he never said a word. He just stared out the window the entire time. His daughter told me he has dementia."

"Oh, that's sad. We learned about that in health class this year," I said. "There are some drugs that can help stimulate the brain, but there's no cure yet."

"That's right, honey. But luckily, this man has a very caring daughter, so he's safe at home."

"Well, that's good. And so is your casserole!" To prove my point, I made a big show of enjoying another bite.

"I agree!" said Darren. "It's delicious."

"Thanks, kids. Best part is, I get to do it again next week. Same time. Same route. Same fee."

When we finished dinner, Dad surprised us with an ice cream cake. I couldn't remember ever seeing him this happy.

Sunday, July 27th

Darren and I met at my dad's house before the next game. I had a plan.

"Something's been bugging me," I said, as we indulged in our pregame snack of popcorn and root beer.

"Oh, yeah? What's that?" His cheeks were so full I could barely understand him.

"Haney was all 'rah-rah, let's figure this out together' until our last visit with him, and then he turned to stone. Come to think of it, as soon as we mentioned Oscar Henderson, Lamont Porter, and Henry Calloway, he didn't say another word."

"I noticed that, too. All the other names didn't matter, but those seemed to touch a nerve." Darren took a long draw on his soda and I braced for the aftershock, but there was none. Yet.

"I searched everywhere on the Internet for the names on our list. Zilch."

Finally, Darren let out an epic belch. With pipes clean, he raised a finger to make a point. "We need to see this Flash guy again. Unfortunately, we're not allowed on the field after the game anymore."

"I know. My new plan is to go *before* the game. I was thinking about this last night while I was surfing the web for info on the Blue Barons. We *assume* they come out only after the game. But why shouldn't they be there before the game? Or even during the game? They're slightly visible at night because there's nothing else to see. Maybe we don't notice their ghostliness during the day, but they're there all the same."

Darren stretched his legs, planted his stocking feet on the coffee table, and laced his hands behind his head. This was how he did some of his most creative thinking. His head started slowly moving up and down and then became a full-blown nod. "That makes sense, April. We should be able to check out their game any time, like . . . after batting practice."

"Exactly!"

"Money!" he said, with a loud clap.

I hate it when he steals my lines.

* * *

After we arrived at the stadium, I picked up the bats from the equipment manager and placed them in the bat rack. The visiting team wanted to take care of its own bats (couldn't blame them for not wanting a twelve-year-old they'd never met to sort their precious lumber), so Darren helped me. It was an easy task, and we were just stalling until the moment was right.

After batting and infield practice, the teams left the field to change into their game uniforms. The grounds crew was busy moving the batting cage and getting the infield ready. No one seemed to notice or care about what we were doing. It was time.

Darren joined me in the Harpoons' dugout and we moved to the quiet corner near the bat rack. "On the count of three," I said. We took out our shadow balls. Once again, the shadow game was in full swing. The Blue Barons were out on the field, so the dugout was almost completely empty— except for the manager, who was at the far end swearing at an umpire. Apparently, some things haven't changed in baseball. The batter for Providence struck out to end the inning, and the Blue Barons came running in.

"Now what?" Darren asked.

"We find out what we can."

Two players came over and got bats from the bat rack. One headed to the plate and the other to the on-deck circle. Flash, who was up third, came over and found his bat. He saw me.

"Hey! April the bat girl, right?" he said.

"That's right. And this is my friend, Darren. He's a bat boy."

"Well, Darren, it's a pleasure to meet you."

"Hi, Flash," Darren said, a little louder than he needed to. He stuck out his hand. Flash shook it heartily.

"It's nice to meet two young people who love the game so much," he said. "I don't know what it is about baseball, but when spring comes, everything seems possible. People are filled with hope and excitement. I just really come alive out here, you know?"

Darren and I smiled at him. "We feel exactly the same way. There's no other place on earth like a ballpark."

"No other place *I'd* rather be," Flash said.

When it was his turn to bat, he stroked the first pitch to the gap in right center and began running the bases. With his blazing speed, he headed to third without slowing down and had a stand-up triple. The throw got away from the third baseman, and Flash went in to score. He wasn't even breathing hard when he returned to the dugout.

"Hey, Flash," I said. "Do you mind me asking how old you are? You look like a real veteran out there."

"Yeah," Darren added. "Like you've been playing for years."

Flash scooped up his glove and cap from the bench. The next batter had made the third out and the inning was over. I thought he wasn't going to answer, but he stopped at the

71

top step, turned around, and smiled. "Same as my number." Then he jogged out to right field—but not before we were able to see the number on his back: 20.

Okay—another piece to the puzzle! Oscar Henderson III was twenty in the year 1940 or so. It was time to go, so I turned towards Darren, but he was standing in front of the third-base umpire, making believe he was arguing with him, getting up on his toes, right in the ump's face. He even kicked dirt on him, like a real major-league manager. The ump saw the dirt on his shoes and shook it off, then walked away and got ready for a new inning. Fortunately, he couldn't see him—or me, for that matter, when I clutched Darren's arm and led him back to the dugout, still kicking and screaming. It was definitely time to return to the real world.

16

Sunday, July 27ᵗʰ

"Man, that was fun!" Darren said. "I *love* being invisible."

"Wouldn't it be great if you could do that any time you wanted? I mean, think of the possibilities!" I pictured Darren kicking dirt on the ump and burst out laughing.

"What?" Darren asked.

"Nothing. You just crack me up sometimes, that's all."

"Hi, you two!" Cannon's voice boomed. "What's so funny?"

"Oh, hey, Cannon," I said. "Nothing, nothing . . . a silly joke—that's all." Darren scampered up the stairs and ran to the other dugout.

Cannon placed a bat in the rack and a helmet in the box above it. "Thanks again, April. That T-ball drill was a lifesaver. Who knows? I may make it to the majors, after all!"

"With a batting average of .400, I'd say it's a sure bet. I really hope you get your chance, Cannon. Meanwhile, I hate to rain on your parade, but I've noticed a small problem with your footwork at first base."

"What's wrong with my feet?"

"Grab your mitt and I'll show you."

He could have danced a waltz by the time I was done with him.

* * *

A hard-throwing pitcher named Jimmy Baxter had recently joined the Harpoons and was making his debut this afternoon. At six-foot-five, two hundred and twenty pounds, everyone called him "Moose."

I watched him carefully and noticed a pattern in his pitching motion. I could tell which pitch he was going to throw by watching his body language. This was something the manager had to know.

"He's tipping his pitches, Skip," I said, as we watched the warm-up tosses in the third inning.

"What?" Smiley said. "That's impossible. The pitching coach has been working with him for two weeks."

"He gives it away every time. Watch."

He rudely moved up a step to ignore me. I was going to have to prove it to him. I started predicting each pitch Moose threw.

"Fastball!"

Fastball.

"Curve!"

Curve.

"Slider!"

Slider.

That got Smiley's attention. "Okay, April, how did you do that?"

"I told you. He's giving it away. Watch his eyes, Skip. For a fastball, he looks straight ahead, but then he peeks into his glove for a curve ball. His slider's harder to pick up, but watch how he looks away as he re-grips the ball. It's a dead giveaway."

We watched the next few pitches and Smiley realized I was right. He called timeout and had a quick chat with Moose.

"Eyes on the prize," he said, as he bounded down the steps. "Moose needs to keep his focus on the catcher—and only the catcher. He'll work on it. Thanks, April."

I beamed, but just a little bit.

"Say, how'd you get so smart, anyway?" Smiley asked. "I know coaches who've been in the game for years who don't pick up on stuff like that."

I wanted to tell him that I tried playing softball but didn't like it much—that I prefer to watch and learn; that I've been posting on baseball message boards for years, and no one's ever guessed that I'm a kid; that my bookshelf is filled with information about every aspect of the game, from biographies to sabermetrics. I wanted to say all that, but I didn't. Instead, I said, "I guess I just have an eye for it, Skip."

Moose plunked the next batter in the ribs, putting the tying run on base. Smiley removed his cap and smacked it against his knee, swearing before he could stop himself. Then he gave me a dirty look.

"Get back to your spot, please."

Sunday, July 27th (After the game)

Darren and I shared a bag of popcorn on the drive home. We brainstormed the encounter with Flash to see what we could come up with.

"Okay," I said. "So Oscar Henderson III was born sometime around 1920."

"That's true," Darren replied. "But that's not much to go on."

"I know, I know. I was just hoping that if I said something out loud, maybe we'd get some inspiration."

"I got nothin'," Darren said. "Perspiration, definitely, but not much else."

Our conversation was interrupted by Manny tapping on the Plexiglas.

"Excuse me," he said, sliding the partition all the way open and peering at us from his rearview mirror. "But I can't help hearing what goes on back there from the driver's seat. I have something I think you two might find interesting." He spoke with an accent but was easy to understand.

He handed us a newspaper. "Page three."

As I looked at Manny's reflection in the rearview mirror, I could tell from the crinkling around his eyes that he was smiling.

"Thank you. What's on page three?" I asked, unfolding the paper.

"You'll see when you get inside," Manny said, as he pulled into my driveway.

Darren and I couldn't jump out of the car fast enough.

Back at headquarters (on the couch), I spread the newspaper out on the coffee table and turned to page three.

"What is it?" Darren asked.

"I'm looking."

There was an article there about the new elephant at the zoo. Not relevant. A bond to fix the school buses passed unanimously. Who cares? Aha! At the bottom of the page was a piece about a local man who'd had a brief stint in the major leagues back in the early 1950s.

"Found it!" I said.

Darren scooted closer and began reading out loud. "'Marcus Mayfield played for the New York Giants for part of a season sixty years ago. He and his granddaughter are auctioning off some of his memorabilia to support a community scholarship program.' And why do we care about this?" Darren asked. "Besides the humanitarian part."

"He played for several years in the Negro Leagues," I said, still scanning the article.

"Yeah, and . . ."

"Maybe he knows about Oscar 'Flash' Henderson III, and/or the Blue Barons, and/or just about anything else we're searching for."

"You know what? We should go talk to this guy."

"Great idea, Darren." You had to love him.

*　　*　　*

I had never been to an auction before. The Harpoons were off tonight—having played their day game—and won!—before a sell-out Sunday afternoon crowd, so the timing couldn't have been better. Plus, Dad was still home, which meant that Darren and I potentially had a ride to the hotel ballroom where the auction was being held.

"Hey, Dad," I said. The TV was tuned to the MLB Network and he was in maximum relax mode in his La-Z-Boy. His six-foot three-inch frame was fully reclined, the footrest was elevated, his remote was in his hand, and he had a half-eaten turkey sandwich waiting on the table beside him. I'd have to bring my "A" game.

"Hi, honey."

"What are you doing tonight?"

"I'm on call. Why?"

"Have you ever heard of Marcus Mayfield?"

"Baseball player, right?"

"Yep. Half a season for the Giants. World Series ring for his efforts. He's auctioning off some of his mementos for charity. I thought you might appreciate what he has, like a bat from the 1954 World Series . . ."

"So you're saying you want to go to this auction and you want me to take you?"

"Well . . . Darren, too."

"Of course." He glanced at his watch. "I'm probably not going to be called now, anyway, so—"

"Thanks!"

Fifteen minutes later, we were heading down the road to the Hampton Inn on Route 6. We snagged a spot near the entrance. Once the car was in park, Darren and I sprinted towards the door.

"Wait for me," Dad said. He's a speedy walker, and I usually have a hard time keeping up with his long strides, but tonight, I'd gotten a head start.

We entered the hotel and followed the signs for the auction. Just as we were pulling open the large double-doors to the ballroom, Dad's phone rang. He held up his index finger and walked down the corridor. Darren and I peeked inside and saw the auction items on display throughout the room. There were photos, baseball cards, uniforms, and, of course, the World Series bat. It was already crowded, as the auction was scheduled to begin in about thirty minutes.

Darren tapped me on the shoulder and pointed over to my dad, who was seated on a bench. His free hand was flapping in the air. Then he stopped, nodded his head, and turned off the phone. He waited another few seconds before returning.

"Sorry, April. I have to go to the airport. Mr. Haney flew back into town tonight and he needs a ride home."

"Can't someone else do it?" I asked.

Head shake. "I'm on call, which means I have to go. This is what happens when you're the low man in the company. And I don't think Mr. Haney would take kindly to my stranding him at the airport." He put his hand on top of my head. "The timing stinks, I know. I'll make it up to you. Promise."

I couldn't help wondering if Haney had done this on purpose to interfere with our plans. But how would he have known about the auction? And why would he suddenly be against us? Whatever the answers, this was a major opportunity wasted.

*   *   *

The trip to the airport and back is forty-five minutes, tops, so Dad dropped us off at home and let us stay there alone while he was gone. We spent our time watching a baseball game and eating everything in sight.

"All righty. What's the plan now that we've missed the auction, April?"

"I'm working on it. It sure would have been great to meet Mayfield, though. He sounds like a true local legend."

"Why don't you contact the granddaughter?"

"Because I don't have her name or her email address. That's why."

Darren smirked his dangerous smirk, the one that meant he knew something I didn't.

"It's Olivia Coiner and her address is ocoiner54@dmail.com. Do you want her phone number? It's 774—"

"Wait a minute. How do you know this?"

The smirk returned. I was too far away to smack him and I had no small objects to throw at him. The paper Manny gave us was still on the table. He tossed it to me. "It's in the article, April."

I opened the paper and flipped to page three. But I didn't see an email address or a phone number. "Where?"

He turned the paper over to the back page and pointed to the corner. "There."

It was a continuation of the piece. The final sentence had everything we needed.

"Okay, then—what are we waiting for, Darren? Let's contact her!"

Sunday, July 27ᵗʰ – Monday, July 28ᵗʰ

I pulled out my laptop, and Darren and I composed an email to Olivia Coiner:

Dear Ms. Coiner,
My name is April O'Day, and I work for the New Blackburn Harpoons as a bat retriever. I also consider myself a student of baseball and would love to learn more about your grandfather, Marcus Mayfield. I was hoping to meet him at the auction tonight, but circumstances prevented me from attending. I have some questions about the Negro Leagues, as well as life in the major leagues. Please let me know if it would be possible for me to contact him directly.
With thanks,
April O'Day

As the auction was probably still in full swing, we knew it might be a while before Olivia responded to us, so we decided to "meet" Marcus Mayfield online. We didn't have the luxury of finding everything in one place, like a fan page, but we did find lots of interesting articles here and there.

"Really impressive," Darren said. He was using Dad's computer to read, while I was searching on mine. "Marcus was quite the man back in 1950."

"You're right," I said. "Here's an article about him from the newspaper archives. The author says he was the most promising young baseball prospect New Blackburn had ever seen. Unfortunately, the opportunities for African-American players were very limited back then."

"Man! That must have been incredibly frustrating for him." Darren was silent for a moment. "At least he got a chance to play in the bigs."

"Some chance," I answered. "Says here he fought in the Korean War and returned with a bum knee. Three months in the majors was all he got, thanks to an injury that never fully healed."

My dad's car rolled into the driveway, so Darren logged off his computer. Dad didn't mind me using it on occasion, but it was best if he didn't know Darren had been touching his keyboard. We found a baseball game on the MLB Network.

"Hey, how's our old friend Mr. Haney?" I asked, as he made his way to the kitchen. Dad headed straight to the refrigerator for the other half of his turkey sandwich.

"He's fine. He was down in Florida on some business." He opened a water bottle and leaned against the counter.

"Did he ask about us?"

"No, I'm sorry. He spent the entire ride on his phone."

Well, it was worth a shot.

"I'll be in the den," Dad said. "Darren, since you don't have your bike, please let me know when you'd like a ride home."

We heard his TV roar to life a few seconds later. Darren's mom had already arranged to pick him up, so we had no reason to disturb the alpha male in his man-cave.

An hour later, we heard the "ding" of an incoming email on my laptop. I popped it open and saw the reply from Olivia:

Dear April,
Thank you for contacting me. It is a pleasure to hear from fans of Marcus's, both young and old. Although I would have enjoyed meeting you at the auction, I'm afraid

Marcus is no longer able to attend most public gatherings. I'm his caregiver, and I would be happy to pass on any questions, especially about his life in the Negro Leagues. He is confined to a wheelchair and suffers from dementia, but his memories for the details of that era are impeccable. I look forward to your questions.
Sincerely,
Olivia Coiner

I had to read the message twice to believe it. Free access to Marcus Mayfield! What an awesome turn of events.

"What should we ask first?" Darren said, still looking over my shoulder at the email message on the screen.

"I'm not sure. I've got about a gazillion questions in my head. You start. I'll type as we talk." By the time Darren's mother rang the doorbell, we had a great list.

Our email went out later that night. The first two questions were . . .

Did you ever play ball in this area?

Do you remember a team called the Blue Barons?

Olivia got back to me within ten minutes and said she would relay the questions to her grandfather. She also said it probably wouldn't take long for him to answer these and to please feel free to send more.

*   *   *

Monday, July 28th

I checked my email every minute the next day but got nothing else from Olivia. Finally an email arrived, but it was just Darren, saying, "Step away from the computer and put on your uniform."

Oh, yeah, the Harpoons! How could I have forgotten about that?!

19

Monday, July 28th – Wednesday, July 30th

An email from Olivia "dinged" just as Darren and I walked through the door to my dad's house:

April,

My grandfather was thrilled to hear from you. He was wondering if you were some sort of a reporter, but I told him you were on staff with the Harpoons. I showed him a picture of you from the team's website and it made him even happier. Here are the answers to your questions (I tried to quote him as accurately as I could):

Q. Did you ever play ball in this area?
A. Yes and no. I played most of my Negro League career for the Cleveland Hawkeyes. But over the years, we traveled now and again to New Blackburn, so some of the locals saw me play. I was just about to head to the Providence Grays when I got the call to the major leagues.

Q. Do you remember a team called the Blue Barons?
A. Yes. They were a little bit before my time. But I heard some of the other players tell stories about them. They weren't in any kind of league. They were what we called barnstormers. They played teams across the country, including—during the off-season—white major-league and minor-league teams. And believe me, they won more than they lost!

April, he had a huge smile on his face the entire time. He loves talking about baseball and the old days, and he wants to hear from you again. Keep 'em coming!
Best,
Olivia

"*Barnstormers,*" I said. "I should have known."

"Maybe that explains why we couldn't find them!" Darren said. "I mean, the record books aren't exactly filled with stats on barnstorming teams."

On the printout filled with all of our questions, we crossed out the first two. "Olivia says he's happy to answer, so let's send him some more questions." I typed up some general questions about his playing days, but one was more direct: *Do you remember a player named Oscar 'Flash' Henderson who played at least one season for the Blue Barons?*

I hit "send." The reply came the next morning:

April,
I have not seen my grandfather this happy in years. He has answers to all of your questions, but he would like to meet you face-to-face. He would love for you to visit and talk some old-time baseball. He doesn't often grant these types of interviews, so I encourage you to take him up on this offer. Please respond for details.
Warmly,
Olivia

A chance to meet Marcus Mayfield?! How amazing was that?

Darren read the message and then made an exaggerated throat-clearing noise.

"Do you need a cough drop?" I asked.

"Nope. I'm good."

"Well, then, what's your schedule like this week?" *Did he really think I'd go without him?*

He swiped open his phone. Acting like a hotshot businessman, he made an imaginary call. "Gretchen, clear my schedule for the week." Then he turned it off and slicked his hair back. "I believe I can squeeze in a trip to see a legendary ballplayer."

I emailed Olivia and told her I'd love to meet her grandfather. I mentioned that Darren, my friend and co-bat retriever, would also like to come if it was okay with her—and my dad, too (especially since he was our ride).

We arranged to meet the great Marcus Mayfield the following day at ten.

* * *

I thought our destination would be a nursing home or an assisted-living facility, but Marcus still lived in the house he'd bought more than fifty years ago. We pulled into the driveway and parked behind a red sports car. Olivia's, probably. She opened the front door to greet us.

"I'm *thrilled* you're here," she said. She was younger than I'd expected—in her mid-twenties, tops.

After introductions, she led us into the house. "He's a little hard of hearing, so don't be afraid to speak up. His memory is mostly intact, but don't worry if he forgets something. Usually, we just move on. If it gets too difficult, though, he becomes frustrated and that'll pretty much end the visit."

She escorted us to a back room where Marcus was waiting in his wheelchair. He still had a lot of hair, but it was completely white. "Grandpa, this is April O'Day; her father, Danny; and their friend, Darren Plummer."

"Wonderful to meet you," I said loudly. Marcus had huge arms and catcher's hands, but his grip was gentle.

"Please, come in and sit down," he said. His voice was deep and rich, not an old man's or a deaf person's voice, as I'd expected. Darren and I sat on the leather couch, and Dad chose the chair next to us. Marcus wheeled himself to the center of the room. "Too many years squatting behind the plate has taken its toll on my knees. I was doing well until a few years ago." He smiled and revealed perfectly white teeth, which looked even brighter against his dark skin.

"And what baseball didn't take," Olivia added, "the Korean War did." She set some iced tea down on the table in front of us.

Marcus dismissed her with a wave of his hand. "Our guests don't want to hear about that stuff. They want to talk some baseball. Am I right?"

"Yes, sir, Mr. Mayfield," I said.

He reached down for his baseball cap on the coffee table and put it on his head. "Now, April . . . if we're talking some ball, you have to play by the rules. There are no 'misters' or 'sirs' in baseball, at least not amongst players. You folks call me by my nickname."

"Mayhem," Darren and I said together. We had both read the same article.

"That's right!" He laughed heartily. "Mayhem Mayfield. And if you'd like me to call you by your nickname, say the word."

"Mad Dog!" Darren said.

Seriously? Where did *that* come from? "April is fine," I said.

"Danny Boy," my dad piped up, with a big grin on his face.

"Well, then," Mayhem said. "Now that the ground rules have been established, what would you like to know?" He leaned forward a bit, ready for whatever we had to throw at him.

"I wrote down some questions . . ." I pulled an index card from my back pocket.

Mayhem rubbed his hands together. "Nothin' like bein' prepared."

"Let's start with the ones from my last email: Playing in the Negro Leagues."

Mayhem looked eager to talk. "I was a kid, barely eighteen, in the mid-1940s. And boy, did I get lucky! I played for a winning team—the Cleveland Hawkeyes. In 1946, we captured the American League pennant, finishing with a record of 53-16. That was a great time. On the other hand, through the years, you should know that we did face a tremendous amount of discrimination. Many restaurants and hotels wouldn't serve us or lodge us. Often, we would just eat and sleep on the bus. And after the games, too many times, the white stadium owners wouldn't even let us use their showers.

"But then, the world of baseball changed forever. It was April 15, 1947, and Jackie Robinson shattered the color barrier by taking the field that day with the Brooklyn Dodgers," he said. "We all figured it would just be a matter of time before the best of us made it in as well." He shook his head. "Some did, but too many didn't. Ten years after Jackie, only a dozen or so other players had joined him: Doby, Thompson, Banks . . . the other teams were slow to follow. It was a darn shame. And plenty of our players were now just too old to transfer to the majors. They'd had their day."

I didn't have to ask many more questions. Mayhem spent the next twenty minutes telling anecdotes about his favorite players. He'd probably told the same stories a thousand times before, but you'd never know it. He was fascinating, even if he did forget a detail or two along the way.

Olivia had explained that her grandfather had a better memory for the past than the present. Fortunately, we were interested in learning about the events of seventy years ago—and not what he'd eaten for breakfast that morning.

I tried to make eye contact with Mayhem as he spoke, but I couldn't help being drawn to the wall directly behind him. It was covered with old-time photographs. One of them particularly caught my attention.

"Excuse me, Mayhem," I said, during a brief pause. "Could we check out your photo gallery?"

"By all means, Amy!"

I didn't correct him.

Dad, 'Mad Dog,' and I went over to scrutinize the photo wall, and Mayhem came over to join us. I pointed to a large black-and-white photo at eye level. It was Mayhem in full catcher's gear with two other players.

"Was this in New Blackburn?" I asked. "That scoreboard looks exactly like the one the current owner still has. It's protected by a tarp under the stadium."

Mayhem wheeled a little closer and nodded. "A rare appearance before the local fans: July 16, 1948. That game went sixteen innings. And I *do* remember that scoreboard. It was the biggest one I'd ever seen. The scorekeepers used to wave the numbers to the crowd before putting them up. They put on quite a show at that park."

This seemed the perfect moment for my most important question. "Mayhem, did you ever hear about a player named Oscar 'Flash' Henderson from the Blue Barons?"

Mayhem's head dropped in thought. Then he looked at me and nodded with a knowing gleam in his eye. "I heard stories from some of the older players about the fastest player any of 'em had ever seen. That was him, the player they called Flash. I never knew his real name. He was just Flash to us."

"Do you know what happened to him?" I asked. "Why he never made the majors?"

"Rumor was he never came back from the war. Like—" Mayhem winced. I couldn't tell if it was physical or emotional. "Like so many others."

Olivia stood and approached his chair. "Grandpa, I think it's time to rest for a while."

He made defensive motions with his hands. "I'm fine," he snapped. "I'm waiting for my granddaughter, Olivia. She's bringing me a sandwich."

That was our cue to wrap up our get-together. "Well, we have to be going, but it was fantastic meeting you, Mayhem."

"How about a picture with my new friends?" he said.

"Of course!" Olivia picked up her digital camera from the end table. Then Darren, Dad, and I gathered around Mayhem and smiled.

"Oh, this is a keeper!" Olivia beamed. "I'll email this photo to you later, if you'd like."

"That would be great," I said. "And if it's not an imposition, could I please have a copy of that, too?" I asked, pointing to the photo with the scoreboard.

"Sure thing. I'll scan it for you today."

Mayhem's head drooped as he shook my dad's hand.

"Fabulous to meet you . . . folks," he said. It was clear he had forgotten our names. But that didn't matter.

Olivia offered us a cheerful smile as we walked to the door. I turned to steal one more glimpse of Marcus 'Mayhem' Mayfield. I was glad he'd had such a full life to remember.

Wednesday, July 30, 2014: I would never forget this day.

20

Olivia emailed me three hours later. She thanked us for visiting her grandfather and attached the photo of the four of us, along with a scan of the old photo with Mayhem and the scoreboard. It looked even clearer than the original. I enlarged it as much as possible.

Darren peered over my shoulder. "Those baggy uniforms rocked," he said. "Teams really knew how to dress for success back then."

I wasn't in the mood for a fashion discussion. I was focused on the scoreboard. Something about it kept me glued to the screen. I zoomed in as much as I could. And there it was, on the bottom right-hand corner, clear as day: the number 20 with two bolts of lightning on either side of it. A signature was etched underneath the glyphs, as well, but I couldn't make it out. No doubt about it: We had to get a closer look.

*   *   *

Since I had made a habit of walking beneath the stadium whenever I had the chance, the groundskeepers got used to seeing me there. It paid off when Darren and I headed down the next day. Several workers walked right by us without raising an eyebrow. A couple of them even said "hi."

When we got down there, we immediately noticed that something was different. "Hey, where are all those piles of junk, Darren? The right side of the scoreboard is completely open—what a break for us!"

"Awesome! Okay, this is it. According to the photo we got

from Olivia, Flash's signature should be right down here." Darren pulled up the bottom corner of the tarp, revealing the name and the symbols carved into the original green paint.

"Wow," I said. "Oscar Henderson's number—20. And those are the lightning bolts for 'Flash.' How cool is that?"

"I know!" Darren said. "And April, check this out. There are even more signatures on the side. Lamont Porter and Henry Calloway . . . there're tons of names! Listen, quick, we don't have much time. Let's take some pictures and get out of here before someone catches us."

I stopped gawking and started snapping. When we heard people approaching, Darren lowered the tarp and we hustled back to our respective dugouts.

* * *

The game in Harpoon-world was uneventful, and we lost to an overpowering lefty, 4-1. However, Cannon was still on an immense hitting streak. I was so happy for him. When I went to retrieve my backpack, there was a text message from Dad. He'd never texted me before in his life. It was short and sweet:

picking you and darren up
will explain later

True to his word, Dad met us in the parking lot after we finished our post-game duties.

"Hi, April. Hi, Darren." He opened the passenger-side door for us, like he was still on the job.

"What's going on, Dad?"

He got in and turned on the ignition. "You'll see."

He was grinning as we headed in the opposite direction of home. This was so not like him. Dad was as predictable as the sunrise. I elbowed Darren in the ribs and he gave me a jerky nod. We were both loving this mystery.

"Okay," Dad said after we turned onto the highway. "Here's the scoop. I met a gentleman at the airport today, Jim

Fogel. He's an older guy, probably in his seventies. We started talking and the subject of baseball came up. Naturally, I told him about our meeting with Marcus Mayfield. Turns out he was a scout in the Twins organization in the sixties and seventies and has a wealth of baseball knowledge."

Darren and I couldn't wait to hear more, but for some reason, my dad was content to tap on the steering wheel to the beat of a softly playing song. Why was he teasing us?

"Fascinating story, Dad."

"Hold on. There's more. I asked him about Flash Henderson, and he recognized the name, if you can believe it."

Now we were getting somewhere!

"By the way, you've never told me why you're so interested in such an obscure player like Flash."

I froze for a second and looked at Darren. We certainly couldn't mention the shadow players. "Oh, he's . . . he's just a player we came across in one of my sports books. Interesting, huh?"

"I suppose. Anyway, Mr. Fogel confirmed Flash was a great player—an outfielder with a rifle arm, who could run like the wind and hit for some power. He was probably better than many of the major-league players of his time. Of course, he never got a chance to play in the bigs."

"We already know all of this. Where are we going?"

"Darren," Dad said, "please reach under your seat and pull out a flashlight. It's getting dark. We're definitely going to need it."

Darren found it and, aiming out the window, turned it on, then off.

"Almost there," Dad said, turning down a nearly deserted side street. I figured it wasn't worth asking anymore.

The voice from the GPS startled me. "You have reached your destination."

This was our destination? It was mostly farmland with a small patch of trees on our right. Dad maneuvered the pickup onto a gravel area and put it in park. He retrieved his own flashlight from under the seat and we all got out of the truck.

"What *is* this place?" Darren asked, aiming the beam straight ahead.

"It's a war memorial."

"Are you sure?" I said. All I could see were some random trees on the side of the road.

"I know it seems odd, coming here at night, but I couldn't wait to show you. Besides, you're going back to your mom's tomorrow."

"Okay. So what are we looking for?"

"Well, we shouldn't have to venture too far. Mr. Fogel told me there's a plaque here with many names on it."

I followed Darren as he aimed the light through the brush and the trees. We glimpsed something shiny inside a tall patch of weeds and briars. It looked like a tombstone. I pushed away the overgrowth and Darren shone his light on it. It read:

> *This spot is sacred to the memory of*
> *New Blackburn natives*
> *2nd Lt. Michael Waring*
> *Sgt. Henry Calloway*
> *S Sgt. Oscar Henderson III*
> *Sgt. Lamont Porter*
> *Lt. Robert Corbin*
> *who died when their US Army transport*
> *crashed here on April 14, 1945*
> *They gave their lives for country and humanity*

"They died *here?*" I said.

Dad came over and put his arm on my shoulder. "Mr. Fogel said that these men were returning from a successful top-secret mission. An African-American squadron provided cover in order for the transport planes, carrying an all-white squadron, to rescue the airmen trapped behind enemy lines. It was incredibly dangerous for everyone involved, but hundreds were rescued. The last group of airmen, both black and white, flew back together on this fateful flight." He paused and sighed deeply. "Flash and the others died in the line of duty, just as Mayhem said."

I brushed off as much grime as I could from the face of the memorial and turned on my camera.

"Darren, can you shine your light on the stone?" I said.

He did, and I snapped three shots to be sure I got all the information. It didn't seem appropriate that this memorial was hidden and neglected. These men deserved better.

"We should get going," Dad said. We quietly made our way to the pickup.

I turned my camera on and studied the photos.

Okay, we had more information now. But what did it all mean?

21

Back at my mom's house the next day, I searched for intel about the others listed on the memorial. It was slow going. Internet access was limited due to her lousy online provider. And because most of the names were common, I was getting nowhere. After an hour of fruitless searching, it finally dawned on me to include the rank with the names to narrow down the number of hits.

Bingo!

I found 2nd Lt. Michael Waring and Lt. Robert Corbin in a link on the bottom of the first page. I clicked on it and brought up a web page that listed fallen soldiers from World War II. I was sure I had finally located something about the plane crash that cost Flash Henderson and the others their lives.

Unfortunately, it was a different memorial. There was a picture of a huge granite monolith in a park near New Blackburn's city hall. Oddly enough, we drove by it every day on our way to the stadium, but I'd obviously never paid much attention. I double-checked the list of about twenty-four names but could not find Oscar Henderson, Henry Calloway, or Lamont Porter. That was strange. Why were only two of the names from the crash-site memorial on this larger one? Why were the other three missing?

*   *   *

Two lucky things happened before Saturday's game. First, because our parents couldn't drive us to the ballpark, Manny was our driver; and second, he picked us up early. Darren and I agreed that this would be a great opportunity to make a quick stop on the way to the stadium. As Manny drove, he quietly sang along with the Portuguese music playing on the radio.

"Hey, Manny," I said. "Were you ever in the military?"

His forehead creased and his dark eyebrows nearly touched. "No. Too young for Vietnam and too old for the Gulf Wars." He maneuvered onto the highway and sped up. "How about you, April? You ever serve?"

I caught a glimpse of his grin as he merged into the traffic.

"Good one, Manny," I said. "No, I'm asking because there's a World War II memorial up the road here in the park. The names of the soldiers from this area who fought and died in that war are on it. I'd love to have a look and take a picture for some research I'm doing to prepare for a history class I'll be taking in the fall. It'll only take a minute."

"I'm not supposed to stop anywhere but the stadium."

"Pleeease?"

I put on my best pout face. Manny looked at me and then sneaked a peek at his watch.

"All right. But you be quick, okay?"

He pulled into the park and waited while Darren and I ran to the site. There was a large rectangular stone slab with WORLD WAR II engraved along the top. The soldiers' names were inscribed on a brass plate below that. I pulled out my camera to take a few pictures.

"Hey, April," Darren said from the other end of the memorial. "I found Michael Waring and Robert Corbin."

"What about the others?"

We read every name, but there was no mention of Henry Calloway, Oscar Henderson, or Lamont Porter.

"Check this out," Darren said, bending over a small plaque at the base of the memorial.

*"To the brave men and women who gave their lives
to protect ours. Dedicated on June 14, 1964,
by the New Blackburn City Council."*

Darren didn't read the council members' names out loud, but we both saw the middle one on the list: Walter Haney.

The limo horn honked and we ran to catch up with Manny, who was slowly rolling away. What a jokester. Fortunately, we made it to the game with time to spare.

* * *

"What does it mean, April?" Darren asked as we prepped for the game. I was sorting bats into the bat rack. Darren was rubbing up some of the game balls.

"I'm not sure. Apparently, Mr. Haney was a city councilman back in the sixties. Seems they were the ones who got the memorial built."

"And that's a good thing, right?"

"You would think." I put the final bat in the rack, making sure all the ends were rotated to clearly display the bat sizes. "But I have a feeling this has something to do with what's bugging Haney. I'd love to ask him."

* * *

We finished our pre-game tasks and ran into Beth in the tunnel connecting the dugout to the clubhouse. She wasn't her typical chipper self.

"I have something to show you, April," she said in a gloomy voice.

"What is it?" I asked.

"It's a message from Cannon. He's been promoted to Triple-A for the remainder of the year."

This was *great* news! He'd worked hard to earn this promotion.

Beth unlocked her phone and searched the display. "Let me see if I can get this to play." She fumbled about for a bit.

"Okay, here we go."

She handed me the phone. It was a video of Cannon.

"Is this going? Yes? Okay. Hi, April," he said. "Well, what do you know? Old Cannon got the call to Pawtucket. As luck would have it, we have a ten-game road trip starting tonight in Syracuse. Before I go, I wanted to say thanks for all the hard work you do for the Harpoons, and for all the help you've given me. You know, I've been playing baseball since I was five years old, and I've never come across a baseball mind quite like yours, April O'Day. You understand things that many people who've been around the game for years will probably never know. As I move on to Triple-A ball, I'm going to try to remember what you always say: Don't make this game more complicated than it actually is." He laughed and his face went off the screen, temporarily. "Okay, well, I have a plane to catch. Can you believe it? I'm one step away from 'the show' and I owe a ton of it to you, April. Thanks again—and good luck." The camera phone wobbled a little before refocusing on his face. "P.S. I made something for you!" He moved out of range but quickly returned with a homemade sign that read "MONEY" in huge letters. Then I heard him add, "I'm sure I'll see you again in a decade or two when you're a coach or a manager or something! Okay, well, please take care of yourself." The screen cut to black.

Beth turned off the phone and placed it in her pocket. "I'm truly sorry you didn't have the chance to say goodbye to him in person, April. Things happen quickly around here. I'll email you his video later."

"Thanks, Beth," I said. "I'd really appreciate that." No apology was necessary, of course. Cannon Caswell deserved to be in Pawtucket and I was proud to have played some part in his promotion.

"Okay, dear, well, I have to get back to work. My, it's

been a busy afternoon. I didn't think we'd ever get that crane unstuck."

Darren and I exchanged glances. What was Beth talking about?

"What crane?" Darren asked.

"We brought in a crane to remove some heavy items from under and around the stadium. The old batting cage had to be cut in half before we could lift it out. And that scoreboard barely, and I mean *barely*, fit through the door. That was a close call."

"Scoreboard?" I said. "They removed it?!"

I ran as fast as I could to the area under the bleachers behind first base. I could hear Beth calling my name as she tried to keep up. There was nothing left at the site but the big green tarp.

"Who ordered this? Where is it?" I demanded.

"Mr. Haney, of course!" Beth huffed, brushing the dust from her arms and shoulders.

"Where is he?" I asked.

"Yeah," said Darren. "What's going on?"

Beth crossed her arms and tapped her foot. "You know, I don't like this tone from either of you. Would you like to try again?"

I took a couple of deep breaths and sighed. "I'm sorry, Beth. It's just that I'm a fan of old ballparks, and that scoreboard is awesome. Is Mr. Haney here? I'd like to talk with him, please."

"Me too," said Darren. "If he's available."

"That's better. And to answer your question, I believe he'll be attending the game tonight. Would you like me to arrange a meeting afterwards?"

"Yes, that would be fantastic. Thank you." I hate being artificially nice, like grown-ups seem to be all the time. It makes my stomach hurt.

"I'll see what I can do. No promises." She looked at her watch. "I believe you two are needed in the dugouts. I'll meet you after the game near the home clubhouse. Now get going."

"Thanks, Beth," I said, as we jogged away.

"No promises!" she repeated.

* * *

Darren and I waited outside the clubhouse after the game, which the Harpoons won handily, 11-2. Beth was ending a phone call when she arrived ten minutes later.

"That was Mr. Haney. He's in his box, if you would still like to see him," she said. I could tell she was more relaxed because she was her cheerful self again.

"Thanks," I said.

She led us to his box and waited as I knocked softly before entering. Darren was right behind me. Mr. Haney stood in the front, looking out over the field. I closed the door behind us and we went down to stand beside him.

"They're still out there, Mr. Haney," I said, my arms crossed like his.

"I'm well aware of that, April."

Darren and I took a step back as he turned to look at us with downcast eyes. "I'm selling the team. I'm selling the old scoreboard. I'm selling the stadium. I'm selling everything. That's why I've been out of town. I've been searching for a buyer, and I think I've found one." He spread his hands out wide. "All of this will soon be somebody else's problem."

I couldn't believe it!

"What happened in 1963?" Darren asked, beating me to the important question.

"I don't know what you mean," Mr. Haney said.

"I think you do," Darren said.

"Me too," I said. "You took over the team in February that year. Then what?"

101

"I will not be spoken to in this manner. You don't understand anything."

"You asked us to help you, Mr. Haney," I said. "Remember?"

"That was clearly a mistake. I'm about to fix that mistake. You're both fired."

"What?" I said. "You can't fire us. We're volunteers."

"I can do anything I want. I'm the owner, remember? Beth? Come in here, please."

Beth quickly entered the box. "Yes, Mr. Haney?"

"Please escort these two out of the stadium. They are no longer affiliated with the Harpoons."

She looked at me, then Darren, and then back at her boss. "What? I don't understand."

"He fired us," Darren said.

"Out!" Mr. Haney pointed to the door.

Beth gave us a hurry-up motion out of his box. As I walked past Mr. Haney, I flashed to the first time he'd started acting all strange. It was when we'd told him those three players' names.

I stopped and walked back over to him. "Henry Calloway, Lamont Porter, and Oscar Henderson III," I said. "Why did you leave their names off the World War II memorial?"

He didn't answer. As I closed the door, I watched as Mr. Haney stood there with his back to me, arms folded, looking out over the dark field.

22

We headed towards the parking lot. Beth was silent at first and then stopped before we walked outside.

"Okay, what just happened in there, you two?"

"We asked him about the scoreboard," I said. "And he told us he was selling it along with the team and the stadium."

"Then he fired us," added Darren.

"What?" Beth said. "He's selling the team? This is the first I've heard of it."

"Well, it's true," I said.

She paused for a moment to collect her thoughts. "Okay, I'll investigate that. But why did he fire you guys? I've heard nothing but great things about both of you."

We looked at each other, knowing that neither of us could tell Beth anything important.

"I got pine tar all over the visiting team's helmets and it wouldn't come off," Darren said, holding back fake tears. "Someone must have complained."

"And I put several of the bats in the wrong place," I added, following his lead. "Three guys struck out because of me."

Beth's cell phone rang and she pulled it out of her pocket. It was a quiet night, so I could easily hear Mr. Haney on the other end. Beth listened for a few seconds. "No," she said. "Not yet . . . We're leaving now . . . Yes, I'll see to it. Good night."

She didn't have to say a word. Darren and I swept past her. "We know the way," I said.

When we reached the parking lot, I took out my phone

103

to call my dad for a ride, but it started ringing before I could push the buttons. It was Manny.

"If you want a ride home, be in front of the players' entrance in three minutes—before the players start exiting the building." Then he hung up.

"Come on," I said to Darren. "We have to run over to the players' entrance."

"Why?"

"Manny's going to give us a ride!"

The players' entrance was on the other side of the stadium from where we'd exited. I began to lose Darren after a hundred yards, so I slowed down to wait for him.

"Go on without me," he said, holding his side. "I'll stay and fight off the savages myself. Save yourself, April! Save the children!"

God, he could be annoying sometimes. "Don't quit now, Darren—we're almost there!"

We jogged until we passed the ticket window near the lot. The limo was parked in front with the passenger door open.

"Hurry," Manny said, motioning us with his hand. "Hop in."

Manny accelerated quickly and we were on our way.

"Mr. Haney gave me strict orders not to give you two a ride home," he said. "But when I heard you'd been let go, I couldn't leave you out in the cold. The players' entrance has no cameras and is far enough away that he can't see it from anywhere in the stadium." He gave the rearview mirror an unnecessary adjustment. Then it was eyes forward.

"Thank you," I said.

"Yeah," said Darren, still catching his breath. "You're a lifesaver."

"Hey, Manny," I said after a few minutes, "has Mr. Haney been acting weird lately?"

"Weird? What do you mean?"

"Well, has he seemed depressed, or moody, or just not himself?"

He did the mirror adjustment again. "Hard to say. He has mostly been quiet. But he is mad at you two, this much I know."

"But why?" Darren and I spoke in unison.

"I can't say. But I am sorry you no longer get to be bat girl." His eyes darted over to Darren. "And bat boy."

* * *

Manny dropped Darren off at his house, and when I got home, I found my dad in his man-cave. Usually he was quick to slip into what he called his "comfy clothes" before hitting the La-Z-Boy. Instead, he was still in his driving uniform, pacing the floor while drinking from a bottle of water. He had a deep furrow on his forehead, like he'd been doing some heavy thinking. He made it to the other side of the room twice before he noticed me.

"Dad, you okay?"

His head snapped up as if I were the last person he'd expected to see. Wow, that was some deep thought.

"Oh, hi, April. I'm fine." He started to pace again.

"Darren and I were relieved of our duties as bat retrievers tonight, Dad."

"Yes, I know. Mr. Haney called me. Oh, and he fired me, too."

"What? Dad, why? You're such a good driver."

"Oh, I'm aware of that. He praised me to no end. But then he said that business was slow and he needed to keep his full-time drivers busy, so we part-timers had to go. Strictly business, you understand."

Dad was not an emotional guy, but he was taking this far too calmly, even by his standards.

"And you're okay with this? I mean, you loved driving for him."

He finally stopped pacing and sat down in his chair.

"I'm more than okay, April. In fact, this is one of the best days I can remember. Do you recall that elderly Asian gentleman?"

"The guy you drive around—Mr. Koh?"

"Yes. Well, he passed away last night."

I sat down on the small couch. "What? I'm sorry to hear that, Dad. But . . . why is that a good thing?"

"Let me explain. I drove him three times a week on the same prescribed route. At first, I didn't pay much attention. I simply drove. Later on, though, when we arrived at each destination, I began to notice that his expression would change—he would appear thoughtful or he would smile. He was clearly going down memory lane as he gazed out the window. This afternoon, when I stopped by, his daughter told me what had happened."

I was still waiting for the good news. Dad took a deep breath and continued.

"I expressed my condolences and asked his daughter to tell me about the places on our route. She said one was the engineering firm where Mr. Koh worked for nearly fifty years. In fact, he'd helped design all of the stadium changes for Haney over the years. They were dear friends. Another was the house he and his family lived in before he became too frail to take care of it. And the third stop—the cemetery—was where his wife was buried. And that's when it hit me."

"What hit you?"

"I've been fooling myself and everyone else for years, April." He sat up straight and clenched his teeth.

"How?"

"I never told you this, but I've been on full-time disability since the accident. My doctors were convinced I would someday need a wheelchair, but they were wrong. In fact, I'm reasonably healthy. Mr. Koh's mental state was poor. However, he remembered what was important: his family, his home, and his work. Those small reminders, every week, of what mattered most to him brought him continued happiness." He clasped his hands together. "I need to find that joy again, April. And I started today."

"What do you mean? What did you do?"

"I swung by the Social Security office on the way home and picked up a form to declare myself no longer disabled. I can work like anyone else. Heck, Mr. Koh worked for the same company for half a century. As of next month, I am officially off disability. I'll be earning my living. And, you'll be happy to know, I'm going to be a better father to you from now on, as well, April. I promise."

I couldn't believe what I was hearing. My father was a changed man. "I'm proud of you, Dad," I said, giving him a big hug.

*　　*　　*

Sunday, August 3rd

The next day seemed empty without a Harpoons game to prepare for. I tried to reach Darren—I wanted to tell him about my dad—but he never answered the phone or any of my texts. He'd been acting stranger than usual since the trip home from the stadium. Maybe being relieved of his duties had gotten to him.

Finally, he texted back:

i got the tickets, you get the ride

Huh?

I didn't understand, so I texted him, asking him to explain, but my phone was silent for hours. At last, he called me.

"Darren, what's going on?"

"We're going to the Harpoons game tonight, April. I bought three tickets."

"Three? You, me, and who else?"

"Your *dad!* He's our ride, doofus. You did ask him, didn't you?"

"Not yet. You never explained what you meant. What's going on?"

"You'll see. Pick me up at six. Bye!"

I love a good mystery. And whatever Darren was up to sounded intriguing. But c'mon. Couldn't he give me one tiny detail?!

*   *   *

"Okay, let me see if I understand," Dad said. "The owner of the Harpoons fires us all, and now you want to go to one of their games? Sounds a little bit crazy, April."

"I know it does, but Darren and I still like the team. Besides, he already has the tickets. It seems like a waste not to use them."

I could tell Dad was thinking about it. And after the promise he'd made the day before, I was confident he'd do whatever it took to make me happy.

"Okay, let's go. In fact, we'll top it off with some real ballpark hot dogs."

We left a bit before six and stopped to pick up Darren. When we were finally on our way, he said, "I have news."

"What news?" I asked.

"Mr.-Haney-being-on-the-city-council-back-when-the-monument-was-voted-on-and-then-built news."

I realized we'd never told my dad about our little side trip to the World War II monument. I spent the next couple of minutes filling him in.

"Okay," he said. "Darren, what's the news?"

"My aunt is a member of the city's historical society. I asked her about the war monument, and she made a few calls to some former council staff members and found out the information we needed. You won't believe what they did."

"What? What did they do?" I asked.

"They left off Henry Calloway, Lamont Porter, and Oscar Henderson III *on purpose*—because they were African Americans. All the others were white. In 1963, the city council, including our very own Mr. Haney, voted that way. It was unanimous."

I thought I was going to be sick. "Why would Haney and the others do such a thing?"

"Prejudice and hatred," my dad jumped in. "Two terrible emotions that can lead to disgraceful results, like this one. And it's ironic, because one year after the council voted that way, President Johnson signed the Civil Rights Act that outlawed discrimination. It's sad that we have to create laws to make people do the right thing. The right thing should just be etched in our hearts."

Etched in our hearts. I don't think my dad had ever said anything so poetic. He was changing.

We were quiet for the rest of the ride to the stadium. When we arrived, I whispered to Darren, "So that's why Mr. Haney started acting strange when he heard the names Oscar Henderson, Lamont Porter, and Henry Calloway. He hadn't heard those names in fifty years. Maybe he feels guilty."

As we walked towards the main gate, I thought about what we could do next. Talking to Mr. Haney wouldn't help, that was for sure. Suddenly, I got a brainstorm.

I just hoped we could pull it off.

23

Sunday, August 3rd

One of the good things about arriving at a game early is getting to watch the players warm up and take batting practice. Dad had his ballpark food and was content to munch away and enjoy all the activity from his seat.

"Darren and I are going to try to catch some home run balls in the bleachers, okay, Dad?" I said. "We'll wave to you when we get there." He saluted and started on hot dog number one.

It felt odd to be in the stadium but not in one of my usual hangouts, like the dugout or under the bleachers. The players were milling about, stretching, and taking some swings in the cage. Some of them could have used my help, but, thanks to Haney, they were on their own now.

We passed the bullpen, where the starting pitcher was loosening up, and found a comfortable spot in the outfield bleachers as batting practice continued. A few balls made it over the wall, and some younger kids rushed to grab the souvenirs. We made no effort ourselves. We just wanted a place to talk, away from my dad. I waved to him, as promised.

"Okay," Darren said. "We have to act quickly. I say we rush his box and tell him what we know and feel. He's definitely here, because he's throwing out the first pitch tonight, but who knows how long he'll hang around."

"That's your plan—to rush his box? He'll never listen to us, Darren."

"You have a better idea?"

Another home run ball landed right in front of us. I

scooped it up and tossed it to one of the little kids running around.

"We have to think like ball players. I'm always telling them not to make the game more complicated than it actually is. We need a simple solution. We need a pinch hitter."

"Who'd you have in mind?"

"Flash Henderson."

Darren scrunched his face. "Yeah, April. One slight problem. He's there and we're here." He made a funny circular motion with his hand, but I knew what he meant.

"I've been thinking about this, Darren. If we can go to Flash's time and see him play, there's no reason why he can't come visit us."

"How?"

"The same way we visit him. Now here's what I need you to do . . ."

I spent the next five minutes explaining my plan to Darren.

* * *

We returned to our seats and ate our hot dogs and nachos. Nothing tastes quite as delicious as ballpark food. Dad had already finished his drink, so he excused himself to use the men's room. His timing couldn't have been better.

"Let's call Beth," I said, taking out my phone. I punched in her number and she answered on the second ring.

"Hi, Beth. This is April."

"April, hi. I'm completely swamped at the moment, but . . . oh, well, what can I do for you?"

"I know you're busy, but this is extremely important. Darren and I are here at the park as spectators. We bought tickets and everything. We both feel awful about how things ended with Mr. Haney and want to express our thanks for a great summer and wish him well."

"That's considerate of you, but—"

"We know he's throwing out the first pitch tonight. It's his birthday—he does it every year. When he comes through the dugout afterwards, we can meet him in front of the clubhouse. It'll take two minutes, tops."

"April, I don't—"

"Please, Beth. It'd mean a lot to both of us."

She paused for about five seconds. "Well, okay. Meet me in front of the clubhouse in twenty minutes. I'll clear it with security so you can use the stairwell."

I hung up and told Darren what she'd said. Step one of our plan was so far, so good.

When my dad came back, I gave him the same story.

"Darren and I are going to see Mr. Haney when he's done throwing out the first pitch. We want to clear the air and try to leave on a positive note. We won't be long."

"That's a wonderful idea, honey. Give him my regards."

Wow, that was easy. The "old" Dad would have questioned my motives and made me work for it. This "new" Dad would take some getting used to.

I needed one important item before we saw Haney. Darren and I went through the tunnel, past the food court, and out to the left-field bleachers. Some of the relief pitchers were stretching in the bullpen; others were spitting sunflower seeds. There was a small chain-link fence next to the bullpen with a clear view of the pitchers. I saw Jimmy Baxter warming up nearby. Normally, the players are immune to anything fans say to them from the bleachers. Some of it can be encouraging, but a lot of it is downright mean. I needed to get Jimmy's attention somehow, and fast.

"Hey, Moose, still keeping your eyes on the prize?" I said, referring to the catchphrase we'd coined to help him avoid tipping his pitches. He turned towards me.

"Hey, April, what are you doing on *that* side of the fence?"

"I'm a spectator today. You guys will have to win this one without me."

He motioned to the catcher that he was done, and the catcher walked back to the bench. "Well, we'll try to win the game for you, April!" he called to me.

"That's incredibly nice of you, Moose, but what I'd really like is an autographed ball for my dad. Unfortunately, I don't have a ball or a pen. Can you help me out, please?"

"Be happy to, April. Back in a flash."

He jogged over to the bench and grabbed a marker from the shelf. He chose a ball from a nearby basket, signed it, and threw it to me. "Here you go."

"Thanks, Moose. Good luck tonight, and remember— eyes on the prize!"

Ball in hand, as we headed towards the tunnel, we heard the national anthem.

We paused with our caps off and then sprinted over to the players' clubhouse.

"Okay, Darren, we have the ball for the double-switch. It's showtime."

"Do you really think it'll work?"

"I don't know. But it's our only hope. When I give Flash this baseball, he should be in our time."

"Right. But please, put your shadow ball back in the pouch at the exact same moment. He'll freak out if you aren't by his side."

"I'll remember. And then, when Mr. Haney meets Flash, well . . ."

"Then what?" Darren asked.

"Well, maybe Mr. Haney will finally be forced to face his past."

"It's worth a try, April."

I could hear the PA announcer introducing Mr. Haney for the ceremonial first pitch. We had to move fast.

"Remember, keep Haney *occupied* when I leave to get Flash."

"Got it!"

A few minutes later, Mr. Haney came through the tunnel. We were waiting in front of a small office next to the clubhouse entrance. He stopped when he saw us.

"What do you two want? I thought I made myself quite clear yesterday."

"You did, sir," I said. "But we wanted to tell you no hard feelings, and to thank you for the great opportunity you gave us this summer."

He paused. "Well, that's kind of you," he said, and resumed walking.

"And to ask a favor."

He stopped again.

"I know you're busy, sir." I pointed to the small office nearby. "This won't take long—I promise."

He made three different faces and then, shaking his head, led the way into the room. "This had better be important."

Darren followed behind him and hovered in the doorway. This was the moment to make my move.

"Mr. Haney, there's someone I want you to meet," I said. "I'll be right back!" I ran down the runway towards the field.

"Where is she going?" I heard Haney's voice boom. I hoped Darren could keep him there until I returned.

As I ran down the tunnel, I opened my fanny pack and slipped the shadow ball out of its leather pouch. This part of the stadium hadn't changed over the years, so I knew the Harpoons' dugout would soon transform into the Blue Barons'. If my timing was good, Flash would be there. I saw daylight ahead and hoped for the best.

No Flash. The manager and the coaches were at the far end on the top step, and some of the reserve players were just sitting, bored, on their end of the bench. I scanned the field as the pitcher struck out the batter and the Blue Barons came running in. Flash sprinted in from right field ahead of most of the infielders. He saw me as he came down the steps.

"Hey, April," he said, revealing a dazzling smile. "Good to see you again."

"Thanks. You, too!" Then I winced, giving him my best pout face.

"What's the matter? Are you injured?"

"Yes, I think I twisted my ankle coming down the stairs." I stepped forward and limped. "I need to get some ice and rest it." I limped again, towards the tunnel and, as I'd hoped, he came up behind me.

"Let me help you."

"Well, if it's not too much trouble."

"Goodness, no. Looks like it hurts a lot." With his glove still on, he put an arm around me, and I draped mine over his shoulder.

There was no office in this old version of the stadium, so we walked slowly until we got to what I figured was the approximate spot. I kept a firm grip on the shadow ball. It was time for the double-switch.

"Thank you. This is far enough, Flash. But before you go, could you autograph a ball for me?"

"Sure thing, April."

I handed Jimmy Baxter's ball to Flash and slipped my shadow ball into its pouch. In an instant, I was in front of the office and Flash was there with me, with his baggy uniform and old-fashioned glove. The double-switch worked!

Flash gripped the ball and looked all around. "Wh— what happened?"

"No time to explain, Flash. There's someone I need you to meet." I practically shoved him over the threshold. "I'll hold your glove, and whatever you do, don't let go of that ball!"

Darren was performing some of his announcer impersonations for Mr. Haney when they turned and saw us.

"Walter Haney, I'd like you to meet the one and only Oscar Henderson III."

24

Sunday August 3rd – Monday August 4th

At first, the two men said nothing. Haney checked Flash out, from his old-timer's cap to his 1940s' cleats. And Flash was as serious and wide-eyed as I'd ever seen him. Finally, Flash extended his right hand.

"Pleasure to meet you, Mr. Haney." His expression bloomed into a smile.

Their handshake was slow and easy.

"The pleasure is mine, Oscar." Mr. Haney added his left hand to the top of the handshake mix. He glanced my way for a second. Good—this was making him uncomfortable.

"Thank you," Flash said.

"No, I want to thank *you*, Oscar."

"For what?"

I saw Mr. Haney struggle. He certainly couldn't thank Oscar for his service to the country during World War II. America hadn't entered the war yet. He hesitated. Then his shoulders sagged. "For coming to meet an old man," he said. "I have made some mistakes in my life. And I'm afraid they have affected other people's lives—and legacies—forever."

Flash looked at me, confused, but when he saw the tears in my eyes, he responded. "Forever? Why, there's no such thing, sir. You can't take the measure of a man until his last breath. You're still here, aren't you? There's always an opportunity to make things better. You know, none of us knows what the future holds, but if we always keep tomorrow in mind, then the battle is already won."

It seemed like neither wanted to be the first to let go,

so they released their handshake at the same moment. Fortunately, Flash kept a solid grip on the ball with his left hand.

They stared at each other for several more seconds.

"Time to return to your game, Flash," I said quietly. "Your team needs you."

He walked towards the door but then turned to look once more at Mr. Haney and Darren. I reached for the baseball.

"I'll get that autograph later, Flash."

I took the ball from him and he vanished—just like that, right in front of all of us. I had no doubt that he had returned to the dugout. Who knows what Flash thought had happened. But from where I was standing, it was clear that he had made a connection with Mr. Haney. And I had a strong feeling that their meeting would alter Mr. Haney's—and maybe even Flash's—destiny for the better. Meanwhile, Mr. Haney looked like . . . well, like he had just seen a ghost.

"What happened in 1963, Mr. Haney?" Darren said gently. "Please tell us."

Haney's face was flushed, so I found a chair and placed it behind him. He slumped into it and put his head in his hands, breathing deeply.

"Are you okay?" I asked. "Do you need anything?"

"No, no. I'll be fine. Thank you, April," he said. "I remember it as if it were yesterday. I had recently taken over the team and, soon thereafter, was elected to the city council. I was young and ambitious and eager to see New Blackburn grow and change. Unfortunately, some things couldn't be changed."

"Like what?" Darren asked.

"Everyone thought the city's World War II memorial was a great idea. The war was twenty years behind us and the timing was right. The list of soldiers was typed and ready to be etched into the plate, but some of the names were missing."

"Oscar Henderson, Henry Calloway, and Lamont Porter," I said quietly.

Mr. Haney nodded. "The city council president, Red Cantwell, showed everyone a photo of the plaque at the plane crash site and said, 'those Negroes already have their own damn memorial.' Except he used a word other than 'Negroes.'"

We knew what he meant.

"Why didn't you say something?" Darren asked.

"I tried. But Red told me if I didn't go along, my political career would be over. The money was waiting to be spent, so I voted yes. It was the worst day of my life." The pain was etched on his face. There were deep creases on his forehead and tears in his eyes.

"But you can fix this," I said. "And then maybe you won't be haunted by shadows anymore."

He nodded. "I know I can, April. And I will."

Mr. Haney didn't waste a moment. While we were still in the office, he picked up the phone and dialed the city's municipal planner to leave a message on her voicemail. "Evelyn, it's Walter Haney. I'm calling about the war memorial. Believe it or not, it's still unfinished. There were certain egregious omissions. Specifically, three soldiers' names were left off the plaque. Let's be in touch as soon as possible to discuss how we can rectify this situation."

*   *   *

Not surprisingly, we were reinstated as bat retrievers that evening. And when I told Mr. Haney the story about how my dad had been inspired by Mr. Koh to give up his disability check, he hired Dad back as a driver, complete with benefits and insurance.

He invited the three of us for lunch at his office the next day. Mr. Haney even asked Dad to wear his driver's uniform. When we arrived, we noticed a nice assortment of sandwiches, fruits, and drinks—and Mr. Haney's leftover birthday cake.

"Thank you all for being here," he said, as he guided us to the buffet. "Please help yourselves."

After we filled our plates, Mr. Haney joined us at the table.

"First of all, I'd like to apologize to the three of you for my recent behavior. It was a mistake letting you go, and I am truly sorry to have put you through it." He sipped some water and turned to my dad. "Danny, you're a fine man and I'm thrilled to have you back on my staff. Please understand that I was having some emotional difficulties dealing with the illness and then the loss of my dearest friend, David Koh."

He reached out and shook my dad's hand. "And since you're already dressed for the dance, we just got a call from a party of twelve that needs a ride to the Boston airport this afternoon. Drive carefully," he said, handing my dad the keys. "The stretch limo is out front, ready to go. I'll make sure these two get home safely."

"Thank you, Mr. Haney." Dad shook his hand and headed out.

Of course, Darren and I both knew that the afternoon driving session was a ploy to get Dad out of the room so that Mr. Haney could talk privately with us. After he was sure we were alone, he began to speak:

"Do either of you know the significance of last April sixth?"

"Other than the fact that it was Opening Day at Haney Field? No," I said.

Haney nodded. "Well, it also happened to be the fiftieth anniversary of the city council's unveiling of the war memorial. Yes, the one that left off the names of Oscar, Henry, and Lamont. I was sitting in this very office when a reporter from the local paper called and asked if I cared to comment. It seems I was the last surviving member of that historic council and the final link to its history. As the reporter spoke, the pain and the memories came flooding in. I can't recall what I said to him. All I can remember is thinking that I had to make things right, once and for all. So when we ended our conversation, I called the council. But as the phone rang, I lost my nerve and hung up. That's when the shadow players began to appear."

He stared silently for a moment, so I said, "And that's when you started asking everyone who worked here if they could see them, right?"

"That's right, April. And nobody could until you two came along. Then, when you mentioned Flash Henderson and the names of his teammates and fellow soldiers, Porter and Calloway, I couldn't deny the truth any longer. I knew there was a connection. I thought I could run away from it, but thankfully, I was wrong." He rose and stood directly in front of us. "And because of you two, I have a new purpose. As a successful businessman, I want to use my wealth to improve life for everyone. I'll make it my mission to ensure that all the gains made by and for minorities, especially African Americans, will not be lost to history." When he made another dramatic pause, I put my sandwich down. It seemed as though he had more to say.

"April, Darren." He held our hands in his. "I want to especially thank you for introducing me to Oscar Henderson. He possessed such keen insight for someone his age, and from this day forward I will follow his advice. I will keep tomorrow in mind with everything I do. Because of him, I'll be able to live every day with integrity."

Mr. Haney pulled out a handkerchief and faced the field to wipe his eyes. Turning around again, he nodded and smiled.

"Mr. Haney, I think you're a great man," I said.

"It's truly an honor to know you, sir," Darren added.

"Well, thank you. Thank you both," Mr. Haney said. "And welcome back." Mr. Haney clapped his hands. "We have lots of things to look forward to together—for this stadium, for our team, and, well . . . for all of New Blackburn."

25

Two weeks later, the city held a dedication ceremony for the updated World War II memorial. After some moving words from the mayor, the head of the New Blackburn Veterans Administration unveiled the new plate. It resembled the old one, but it was brighter and the names were easier to read. Everyone in the crowd applauded.

Mr. Haney, looking elegant in his blue suit and jazzy tie, stayed in the back with us, a distance away from the main festivities. Officially, an anonymous donor had provided the new plate, but I'll bet a lot of people knew who was really behind it.

"Mr. Haney, you told me last week that Flash's relatives would be here. Can you point them out to me?"

"Sure, dear. There they are." He directed me to a young couple standing by the monument. "That is Oscar Henderson's great-nephew, Marvin Henderson, and his wife, Sheila. Can you believe they traveled all the way from California for the ceremony?"

"That's fantastic," I said, patting the bag I was carrying. "Please excuse me for a few minutes, okay?"

Darren followed me over to the pair, who had located the name Oscar Henderson III etched in the brass and were taking pictures.

"Pardon me," I said. "Mr. and Mrs. Henderson?"

"Yes," the man said in a friendly voice. "I'm Marvin and this is Sheila."

I gazed down and noticed that Sheila was pregnant.

123

"Hi. I'm April O'Day and this is Darren Plummer. We worked over at the local baseball stadium this summer and we came across something we thought you might like." I opened the bag and removed a baseball glove. "This belonged to your great-uncle, Oscar Henderson III. His nickname was 'Flash' because of his incredible speed. His barnstorming team played in our stadium many years ago."

Marvin accepted the glove and tried it out, pounding his fist several times into the webbing. "Are you sure this belonged to him?"

"Positive," said Darren. "If you look closely, you can see two small lightning bolts surrounding the number twenty drawn on the thumb of the glove. That was his signature marking."

Marvin examined the glove and found the small drawings. "Well, will you look at that? I don't know what to say, other than thank you . . . *very* much. This is really quite remarkable."

Sheila patted her stomach. "I'm sure our son will appreciate having it one day."

Marvin put his hand on hers. "We're planning to name him Oscar—Oscar Henderson IV."

"That's terrific," I said.

We watched as they disappeared into the crowd, admiring their newfound memento. Darren edged closer and I took his hand . . . or maybe he took mine.

"Awesome," he said.

My thought exactly.

26

In the week that followed the rededication of the memorial, change was coming to the ballpark. The team was away for its final road trip, and, according to Joe, things were hopping. He told me that the area beyond the outfield wall was crawling with heavy equipment and workers, but as he'd been sworn to secrecy by Mr. Haney himself, he couldn't tell me more. And since there were no bats to retrieve while the team was away, we were left in the dark.

"Why is Mr. Haney being so mysterious?" Darren asked, as we watched a baseball game at Dad's place. It was day seven of the weeklong road trip.

I turned the volume down with the remote. "I'm not sure. But I *can* tell you this: I can't stand not knowing."

Dad was out on what he referred to as a "short call," meaning he would be gone less than an hour. My phone vibrated on the coffee table and I saw his number on the screen.

"April, I'm going to be home in ten minutes," he said, his voice crackling on the other end. "Get ready, because we've all been invited to the stadium by Mr. Haney."

"We have! For what?"

"I'm not entirely sure. He called me while I was driving back from the airport and said he wanted me to pick you two up. It sounds important."

"We'll be ready."

Dad was closer to home than he'd let on. He rolled into the driveway five minutes later. Darren and I were waiting for him outside and we quickly climbed into the limo.

"He didn't tell you anything?" I asked, buckling myself in.

"No, just that he wants to see the three of us at the stadium—pronto."

Dad drove past the main gate to the players' entrance and parked right in front. Mr. Haney and Beth were waiting at the door.

"I'm truly glad you could make it," he said. "We've been doing some extraordinary things here. It's time to share."

"This way, please," Beth said.

We followed them into the tunnel leading to the dugout. When we reached the top step, I saw it immediately.

The old scoreboard was back—and then some! So *that's* what all the commotion was about.

"Beautiful, isn't it?" Mr. Haney swept his arm towards center field. The old scoreboard had been placed on top of the new one, and the whole thing was, well, perfect.

"Years ago, when I had the workers place that old scoreboard under the bleachers, I buried my past. Or so I thought. Because of the wording in the contract, I had to leave it at the stadium, but it didn't stipulate where, so after the city council voted in 1963, I concealed it as far under the stadium as I could and covered it with anything I could find. I tried to hide the signatures of the men who played in that final Negro League game before World War II—Oscar Henderson, Lamont Porter, and Henry Calloway—the men who lost their lives after that successful mission. But now I can display them proudly because the memorial is complete and correct." He paused for a moment to collect himself. "In fact, we've left the BB's and the Grays just as they were, frozen in time forever."

"Why are you displaying three pairs of teams up there?" Darren asked.

"Ah, good question. The middle two rows are for the Harpoons and the Guests, and the bottom set of rows is for the American Legion and the Babe Ruth teams. They deserve their own digital display as well."

Beth nudged him. "Don't forget about the signs."

"Good point." He tapped a number into his phone. "Joe, light 'er up!"

Within seconds, the scoreboard sparked to life. It displayed zeroes in all nine innings for the Harpoons and the Guests, as well as for the Home Team and the Visitors along the bottom. The BB's and the Grays remained unchanged at 9-3.

"One more thing," Mr. Haney said. "You're going to love this. We're ready, Joe!" Three digital signs lit up next to the three sets of names.

"Honoring Our Past," I said, reading the sign for the Negro Leagues.

Dad read the one for the Harpoons: "Treasuring Our Present."

"Dreaming of a Bright Future," Darren said, pointing to the Legion sign. "That's awesome, Mr. Haney." My dad and I agreed.

"There's more," Mr. Haney said. "Tell them, Beth."

"We'd like to have an old-timers' game here at Haney Field after the season ends. We'll invite all the former players from the area. You'd be surprised how many there are. Plus, we'll have old-fashioned uniforms and mascot races and dollar concessions."

"Dad's a former player," I said. "He was a first baseman in Double-A ball for two seasons."

Mr. Haney patted Dad's shoulder. "Well, what do you think, Danny? Ready to put on the cleats again?"

"No, but I'm honored by the invitation. I'm afraid some of my body parts aren't what they used to be." He reached for his lower back with both hands and winced. "About the only thing I could do is perhaps coach first base."

"Consider it done."

"And as for you two," Beth said to Darren and me, "we have something special in mind to utilize your unique talents."

"I'd be thrilled to be a bat retriever at the old-timers' game," I said.

"Me too," Darren added. "I would rock in one of those baggy uniforms."

Mr. Haney laughed. "I don't doubt that, Darren," he said. "But no, you and April are far beyond fetching bats. How would the two of you like to be assistant managers? You'll get to help choose the lineups, make the pitching changes, and control the game, just like any other baseball manager. Interested?"

I couldn't believe what I was hearing, and neither could Darren, apparently, based on his stunned expression. I tried to talk, but what came out sounded more like a squeak.

"Is that a yes?" Mr. Haney asked.

I turned towards Darren and we both nodded and said yes in unison. I needed to jump and he needed to jump, so we held onto each other and jumped together. I motioned to Dad and he joined in the jump-fest. Finally, Haney and Beth surrounded us and there we were, five extremely happy people jumping for joy in the shadow of the coolest scoreboard in the country.

A million questions popped into my head, but one stuck out the most. "What are the teams going to be called for this old-timers' game?" I asked.

"Oh, it'll be one for the ages," Haney said. "The home team will be the Blue Barons."

"And the visitors will be the Grays," Beth added. "I heard they were both marvelous teams."

Haney motioned to the sparkly scoreboard. "And as you can see, we're ready to go."

27

The old-timers' game got underway early on a beautiful Sunday evening on the last day of summer. School had already begun, but we raced through our homework most days to help coach the players whenever we could. Baseball was still our highest priority. We managed to find fifteen players for each team, ranging in age from twenty-five to sixty-five. Both the Grays' and the Blue Barons' uniforms were baggy and authentic, right down to the logo, thanks to Darren's perfect recall.

Mr. Haney decided that this game was too special to be missed, so there was no charge to attend. And true to his word, the hot dogs, pretzels, and drinks cost a dollar.

The guests of honor were none other than Marcus "Mayhem" Mayfield and Olivia Coiner. They both threw out a ceremonial first pitch before joining Mr. Haney and his family in the owner's box. Olivia insisted that Darren and I sign the first-pitch balls, but I did one even better by getting all the players from both teams to sign them.

The teams took infield practice, and then Darren and I handed in our starting lineups to the home plate umpire, just like real managers. Soon it was game time!

While the Blue Barons headed out to the field and the starting pitcher (a 45-year-old ex-major-leaguer) took his warm-up tosses, Dad pulled me aside in the dugout.

"This is incredible, April," he said. "I have to hand it to Mr. Haney. When he puts his heart into a project, extraordinary things happen."

"I couldn't agree more, Dad. What a perfect night for baseball."

"In fact, it's the second-best thing to happen to me this weekend."

"Second-best?"

"Yep. Take a gander behind our dugout and tell me what you see."

I walked up the concrete steps and turned towards the crowd. I had to shield my eyes from the bank of lights with my hand, but then I understood, because there was my mom sitting in the first row.

"Hi, sweetheart!" she called, with a wave. "Beautiful night, isn't it?"

"The best!" I smiled and waved to her. "And look, Mom— not a cloud in the sky!"

"We've both been missing each other," Dad said. "So we've been calling one another regularly. If a storm's coming in, I call to calm her down. And after a long day of driving, she calls to see how I'm doing. And, of course, we talk about you, April, a lot. We are both extremely proud of you." He removed his cap and used his arm to wipe his brow. "We can't promise you anything, but we're trying. I thought you should know."

I started to hug him, but then the umpire yelled, "Play ball," so we turned it into a fist bump instead.

Well played, Coach O'Day. Well played.

The game was no thing of beauty. But that didn't matter to the crowd, who cheered every hit, every defensive play, and every strike out. And they hooted and hollered loudly between the sixth and seventh innings when two mascots raced around the perimeter of the field. One was dressed as a shark and the other as a whale. The shark won by a snout.

The old scoreboard served us well as the game went along.

Two of Mr. Haney's great-grandchildren—twins Walter and Cassandra—hung the run numbers after each inning. The green paint really glowed under the stadium lights.

The two of us managed the game well and made sure each player had his turn. Darren being Darren, he got into a small skirmish with an umpire after a close call went our way. It was all in fun, though, and when it was over, the two of them high-fived to the delight of the crowd.

Before the ninth inning, the stadium announcer reminded everyone to stay for the post-game fireworks. I made one last pitching change to close out the ninth and the game ended with a deep fly ball to center field. Not that it mattered, but the Blue Barons won 7-6.

All of the players and the coaches came onto the field to congratulate and hug each other and snap pictures.

Dad caught up with me as we were mingling. "Your mom and I are staying for the fireworks if you want to join us." He waved to her in the stands.

"I'd love to, Dad, right after my interview. A reporter from the TV station wants to talk with Darren and me. Can you believe that?"

"That's great, April." He brought me in close for a hug. "You know where we'll be."

The sports reporter and her cameraman met us out near the pitcher's mound. The light above the camera was super bright, but I adjusted. She asked me simple questions, like how we got the team ready to play. Darren went overboard and answered every question as if he were a real manager in the major leagues. The interviewer was surprised at first, but she caught on quickly. We were both a big hit.

At last, it was time to celebrate. The banks of lights began to turn off one by one, indicating that the fireworks were about to begin. Soon the field was down to a soft glow.

I grabbed a much-needed water bottle from my backpack, tucked in its usual spot in the corner of the dugout. The field had become quiet and dark . . . and that's when I saw it.

A shadow player? Who was still here? I had to find out, so I removed my shadow ball from its pouch. Suddenly, the field was alive with brilliant colors and sunshine. One player was visible. I walked up to the top step to see who it was.

"Hey, April," Flash said as he walked towards me with a warm smile. "Fancy seeing you here again." He checked out my uniform. "And finally looking like one of us, I see."

"Hey, Flash. It's great to see you." No other players were on the field. "What happened to your game?"

"Oh, it ended a while ago. There's a lot of talk that we'll be going to war soon. So I just thought I'd stop by for one last look. I don't know when I'll be back."

His face was beginning to fade away—and the shadow ball was growing fainter—so I knew I didn't have much time. "I'm glad we got to see each other again, Flash. It was a pleasure getting to know you."

"The pleasure was all mine, April O'Day."

Before Oscar Henderson III and the daylight faded away for good, I pulled him in close for a big hug.

I hugged him for his family, who would miss him terribly; for the friends he'd be leaving behind; and for the world that owed him so much. I hugged him extra hard for me—to remember the hero I'd always carry in my heart.

We stepped back from one another and smiled one last time, and then he was gone. After a few moments, I looked down at my empty hand. The shadow ball had vanished, too.

*   *   *

Back in the stands with Darren and my parents, with the trace of a breeze carrying our oohs and aahs, I watched as the fireworks lit up the sky and rained their dazzling colors upon us. I glimpsed Mayhem and Olivia in Mr. Haney's box, smiling at the spectacular display.

And all I could think was that the world would never be as beautiful as it looked tonight at Haney Field.

Acknowledgements

I'd like to thank everyone who worked so hard to get this book ready for publication. Kudos to publisher Margie Blumberg, who saw magic in these pages and helped transform them into something truly special. I applaud editors Emma Walton Hamilton and Elizabeth Bernstein, whose knowledge and skill made this a better book. Well done! Many thanks to graphic designer Joseph Gisini of PageWave Graphics for the wonderful cover and the interior design. I am grateful to my beta readers—Kim Cogburn, Kelly Andrews, Jenna Nelson, and Sandra Clark—for putting up with some early drafts and short deadlines. Your help was priceless. Heartfelt thanks to my agents, Jenn Mishler and Fran Black, for sticking with me through the dark days. And best wishes to my Internet supporters: The Bored, Purgatory, Pitizens, and Ynots. Thank you all!

Made in the USA
Charleston, SC
06 December 2016